The Jew

The Jewel of the Glen

~~ The Glen Highland Romance ~~
4

Michelle Deerwester-Dalrymple

ISBN: 9781709217227

Chapter One: The Return of the King

HIS FEET SUNK into the sandy bottom of the unforgiving Little Minch, icy waves lapping against his boots as he strode to shore. Months had passed since he last laid his doe-brown eyes on his beloved Highlands, but his time in hiding had to come to an end. 'Twas time to return, face his enemies, and secure the sanctity of his crown.

Robert the Bruce hated that he had to secret his kingship on a rock in the middle of the sea after the death of John Comyn. He feared his following may have waned, that the English had gained a stronger foothold in Scotland, or God-forbid, managed to usurp his crown altogether.

The desire to safeguard his position as King and create a unified Scotland burned deeply in him, heating his body against the cold waters. His water-logged boots left footprints on the sand, as though he was a mysterious Blue man, emerging from the sea, ready to command the life and death of men. The Bruce watched as the stony-gray waves crashed ashore, rolling over his footsteps as if he had never been there.

That would not be his legacy in Scotland. His strength as King, and thus the strength of Scotland, would not be denied.

His men shivered as they walked up the narrow beach, while the rest of his coterie pulled the boats to the shore. Many men from North Uist, including several from both the MacDonald and MacRuaidhrí clans, rallied to his call, shoving each other aside to be the first in the boats heading to the Highlands. Pride swelled in the Bruce's chest at their eagerness. How could he refuse these men the leadership, the Scotland, for which they fought so long and hard?

He had been surprised at the sheer number of men who volunteered to join him on his trek over the Minch. There was an excellent chance they may never see their beloved island again, yet they convened, nonetheless. Dougie of Clan MacDonald was one of the first to join the Bruce, an action that did not surprise the Bruce in the least. After his troubles on North Uist, trying unsuccessfully to have a local woman and her sisters tried as witches, Dougie needed an escape. Taking up the banner of the King of Scotland was a strong option. And though Dougie had a modicum of power on the isle, he was a man too large for such a small island — a voyage to the Highlands would do the man well.

Once the Bruce reached the dry grasses of Malliap, just south of the Highlands proper, he paused. The sight of the grasses in the glens, the snowcapped mountains, the expanse of pristine land to which none other compared, filled his view. Scotland was God's land on earth, Robert the Bruce was convinced, and he would defend it to the death. He inhaled the crisp air, collecting his thoughts. 'Twas time to institute his strategy, rout the English, and unite his country.

His men collected on the grass behind him, wiping at their wet breeches with handfuls of dry grass. The Bruce had no patience for such trivialities as wet pants.

"My good countrymen! 'Tis time to take back our country from the English and those who would support them. For Scotland!" he called, and a rousing cheer erupted from the men. "I need five men to volunteer, messengers to run in each direction across Scotland to make all the clans aware that their King has returned."

***

The need to rally the clans smoldered at the forefront of the Bruce's mind. 'Twas early spring and snows were beginning to melt. Too soon the English would ride north and, with the backing of many lowland clans, challenge his crown. He hoped his messengers would be swift of foot and that the announcement of his return would spread like wildfire through dry grass.

With the clansmen who remained on the narrow shore, he directed them to head north with him, riding for clans friendly to the Scottish crown and eager to throw off the bitter English mantle once and for all. Of the clans, including the powerful Douglas clan to the south, the Bruce knew he must reach out to his most loyal compatriots first. That meant riding north of Castle Inverlochy from Cameron's lands, past the MacKenzies, for the man who risked his life to ensure Robert escaped the Battle of Methven and the commander of the English contingent in Scotland, the Earl of Pembroke, Aymer de Valence. That Scotsman's actions, even up to slapping the hindquarters of his frightened horse, had assured the Bruce's safety. The man was the reason Robert the Bruce was stepping on Highland soil once more.

The MacCollough stronghold lay to the northwest of Inverlochy, and the Bruce owed the young Laird his life. He was a faithful supporter, and Robert wanted to knight the lad and acknowledge him as a close adviser before he rallied the Highland clans and pushed south into the traitorous lowlands. So much of the lowlands was entrenched with English and their supporters— not the least of whom was Comyn's brother-by-law, the Earl of Pembroke. Robert's face burned with frustration at the thought of the Comyn and Balliol legacy and how they nearly cost Robert his crown.

BlackBraes stronghold was the first stop he would make as his army marched across Scotland. The journey north would be long and cold, especially if a local clan didn't grant them horses. But the Bruce had slogged this far to Scotland that walking through the moors to the foothills of the Highlands was no impossible feat. If anything, 'twould help him reconnect with his beloved homeland.

They were fortunate; a tacksman of Laird MacDonnell of Glen Garry encountered them while they were still far west and commandeered several horses from the locals. The tacksman told King Robert he wished he had more horses as many men were still trekking on foot, but the men wanted the Bruce to ride and find his man.

Sharing a meal of dried haddock and oatcakes with the tacksman at the village inn, a run-down building near the center of the village, gave the Bruce time to learn as much as possible of the events he missed in his absence. They shared mead, and after directing his men to head north to Clan MacCollough, Robert mounted his new steed and rode off, four of his advisers riding alongside. Excitement to gather at the Laird's stronghold rippled among the men.

'Twas only a few days later when King Robert and his small royal party trotted to the MacCollough lands. Several MacCollough men stopped the riders in the woods, only to cheer madly at their introduction to the King of Scotland himself. They joined the King's men, riding at the back, as escort for King Robert into MacCollough's inner bailey.

MacCollough kinsmen and women raced to the riders, calls of "huzzah" and "hail to the King" echoing through the glen, announcing the arrival of the King of Scotland.

As for Laird Declan MacCollough, he had snuck away from his duties to attend his wife, his magnificent Elayne. Though married for several months, they behaved as newlyweds — taking every opportunity to meet each other, joining hard and fast before resuming their chores. More than once they scrambled to adjust their plaids while clansmen beckoned. This time, Declan lifted his head off his wife's breast at the cacophony in the yard.

"What is it, my husband?" Elayne sat up onto her elbows as Declan turned his ear to the window slit.

"I dinna ken," he answered, disconcerted. W*hy had his men not roused him? What was the chaos in his bailey?* He had believed he and Elayne had put a stop to such improper behaviors on the part of his men. What caused them to behave like wild animals again?

The cheering only grew louder as Declan wrapped his tartan around his shoulders and rushed past the chamber door. Elayne MacNally MacCollough readjusted her shift and grabbed her own fur-lined cape to follow her husband outside.

***

A small ensemble of men rode into the yard, a handsome man with a brown beard just starting to show gray highlights dismounted, smiling at the cheers and men who approached him. Some bowed, others jumped, and at the back of it all, Declan MacCollough stood on the steps of his keep, not believing his own eyes. His King, the very man he helped escape from Scotland, had returned to the Highlands.

Elayne crashed into Declan's back, peering around his shoulder, ready to educate the men on their behavior, that proper decorum must greet her guests. At the scene in the yard, however, a shocking event occurred — Elayne lost all her words. Her own jaw dropped when she gazed upon the man standing amid the chaos in the bailey.

"Declan!" she breathed. There was no mistaking the man before her eyes. "'Tis him, aye? The Bruce?"

Declan pulled her in front of him and wrapped her in a bearish embrace, lifting her off the stones. His own cheering rang in her ear, then he almost dropped her as he clasped her hand and dragged her into the muddy yard to meet the King of Scotland.

Chapter Two: But Traitors Remain

THE PAST FIVE months had been rough ones for Gillivry. After Donald Ross and the men who followed him to the MacCollough keep met a surprise attack and were shipped off to stand trial with the faithful MacDonalds, Gillivry Ross realized that heading home to the seat of Clan Ross was a bad idea indeed.

Last year, after their retreat from the failed skirmish with MacCollough on behalf of the English, Gillivry separated from the fractured remnants of the Ross clan. They may have gone back to Castle Ross, and if they did, there was an excellent chance that, if they were not yet guests of the MacDonald dungeons, they would be shortly. Becoming a prisoner of Scotland under the MacDonalds did not fit Gillivry's plans at all.

While he had not agreed with Donald Ross's frenzied machinations against MacCollough personally, Gillivry did agree with Ross's overall stance that England should rule the whole of the isle. Wild Highlanders and bickering nobles had never served the country well; Gillivry knew that as he knew his own hand. He'd seen the benefits of English rule, heard about it from the lowlanders, and wanted to make himself part of that larger enterprise, to continue Clan Ross support.

Returning to the Highlands was out of the question; the Highland clans would kill him as soon as they saw him. But his sister, last he'd heard, lived in Edinburgh with her husband, a tailor, and their children. He had not seen her or spoke to her in years, to be sure — all the same they were family. And he could get lost in Edinburgh until he figured out what his next movement should be.

Gillivry asked around Edinburgh for the home of the Leslie's, and after stumbling over scrambling rats and refuse in the mucky streets, he came across a well-constructed thatched house off the main thoroughfare of High Street. The tailor shop formed the bottom of the house, and a narrow stairwell on the right led to a wooden door — the living quarters.

Climbing the rickety stairs, he'd kept his head bowed against the screaming wind. Winter had been coming upon them strong and hard. He hoped Edinburgh would be a bit more temperate than the foothills and mountains and that his sister and her husband would welcome an estranged family member. 'Twas too cold for him to find shelter elsewhere – moreover, where would he go?

His knock at the door was answered by a short woman whose long, brown hair was bound and covered by a pale head kerchief. Her sallow green eyes looked him up and down with distaste, and Gillivry was certain he resembled more of a wet street rat than a man.

"Weel, if 'tisn't my long-lost brother come to visit me at last," the woman's wry voice did not appear welcoming, but Gillivry didn't let that bother him. He displayed the largest smile he could manage at his sister.

"Dear Mary!" he gushed. "I have no' seen ye in years! Have ye nay embrace for your brother?" He lifted his arms to her. Mary shook her head.

"I kent ye to be in the Highlands, with the Laird. What business have ye in Edinburgh?"

Information did not travel swiftly in Scotland during the winter, much to his delight, and news of the MacCollough attack had not made it to Edinburgh yet. With any luck, 'twould not make it at all. What care did the good men and women of Edinburgh have of a small clan far into the Western Highlands? And if it did, he hoped his name remained unspoken.

"I dinna want to stay in the Highlands," he admitted, presenting the story he'd invented as he traveled. "The Laird of Clan Ross is no' a stable man. I hear he may have been taken prisoner by rogue Highlanders, and I dinna want to reside with such lawlessness. Afeared for my safety, I decided to make the long trek to ye. Perchance your brother may stay the winter with ye? Help your husband in his business? I will no' be a bother, I promise."

Mary knew the value of her younger brother's promises, having seen them broken over and over in her childhood. But her brother was a child no longer. A full man stood before her, a man who might help her husband in his business and mayhap bring in more coin for the winter. Pragmatism won her over, so she shrugged and stepped aside.

"I will have to ask Finlay if ye can stay, if he can use ye in the shop," she explained as she took him to the hearth. Finlay Leslie was nothing if not a shrewd man, and an extra hand to take on more work was something he'd welcome, Mary knew.

Gillivry stuck his nearly frozen fingers as close to the fire as he could without burning the tips. He was chilled to the bone, visibly shaking, and grateful Mary had let him inside. The possibility that he might reside here warmed him as much as the fire.

A slight movement at the corner of his eye drew his attention to a cluster of three young children near the table. A kitchen area had been set up in that section of the room, with several cups and wooden plates stacked on a shelf, and foodstuffs peeking out from a canvas-covered storage bin under the shelf. He presented his most warming smile at the youngsters, but only the baby boy, a child no older than two summers, grinned back.

Mary noticed the interaction.

"My bairns," she addressed the children. "'Tis your uncle Gillivry." They continued their wide-eyed stares. Mary then pointed to each child individually, starting with the eldest. "Peter, Bonnie, and baby Kenny," she told him.

Gill nodded toward each bairn accordingly. Mary moved into the kitchen space, tearing a piece of bread off a dark loaf. She placed it and a hunk of hard cheese on a wooden platter and handed it to him.

"Here. Ye must be hungry. Eat, and ye can speak to Finlay when he comes back from the shop."

Starved, Gillivry tore into the food without responding.

***

Of course, Finlay agreed, and Gillivry spent his winter working as an apprentice to Finlay in his tailor shop. His sister and her husband were kind enough to make a place for him in the attic space of their house, a slender ladder leading through an opening in the floor.

The upper space of the house was low — he had to crouch while up in the attic — and there was a bit of a draft from thinning gaps in the roof, but he had warm bedding and his own space away from children and the prying eyes of his sister. The roof didn't leak, so he kept dry. He was more than grateful to spend the winter in such humble accommodations. Gill knew well enough he may have spent it sleeping outside in the cold.

The work in the tailor shop was tedious, often boring. But 'twas also warm and kept Gill busy and out of the way of the Highlands. Rumors regarding the Highland clans, and of King Robert the Bruce, died down over the harsh winter. More clans believed that he was perhaps no true King, crown or nay, and acknowledging the English lords who began to establish themselves firmly along the Scottish border.

While still far from the borderlands, Edinburgh had welcomed several English lords, and shrewd English merchants who likewise sold English goods. Encouraged by their appearances in Edinburgh, Gillivry made his way toward those shops, striking up conversations to see if he could learn anything about the Ross Clan. From what he could gather, most of his small clan had dispersed, flung into the four winds, his Laird undoubtedly killed by Highlanders loyal to the infernal Bruce.

And he kept his identity secret. What good would come of admitting he was part of that now lost clan? He was able to get by on his first name, for the most part, and if anyone questioned further, he indicated he was the brother of Mary Leslie. If they assumed he were a Leslie, so much the better. He wanted no Highlanders looking for a seneschal of Clan Ross in Edinburgh.

Springtime brought with it crocuses, melting snow, and gossip from the west. While running an errand at the cloth seller for Finlay, one of the English merchants mentioned a rumor he heard of the Highland clans cheering the return of the Bruce King.

"What king?" Gill interrupted. Had the English finally invaded Scotland?

"The Bruce," the merchant said curtly.

Gillivry could tell the man was not pleased. Paying for his items, Gill exited the shop. Instead of returning directly to Finlay, he stepped into the pub at the head of the thoroughfare, looking for ale and more gossip.

He heard nothing of Clan Ross — the emergence of the Bruce from his seclusion was more important news than any other. The word from the pub patrons, many of whom celebrated the return of the pretender, was that the King was traveling across the Highlands, gathering his men, rallying the clans, ready to ride south, rout the remaining English and their supporters, and rule Scotland as its rightful King.

Rightful King, Gill thought dismally. The MacColloughs and their base, animal behaviors showed that the last thing this country needed was a Scottish King. The Bruce's Highlanders stripped Gillivry of his home and his own Laird, and he wanted a hint of his past comfort and security back. He did not think such an outcome possible under a crass Highland usurper. His Laird had the right of it, crazed as the old man may have been, supporting the English claim to Scotland.

Gill struggled with this news. He and his clansmen had been Balliol supporters, then Comyn supporters, under the auspices of the King Longshanks of England. Now that this usurper had returned, thinking he could just stride in and make a grab for the throne, Gill wanted to know as much as he could. Sipping the last of the ale from the mug, Gill considered his next movement.

Staying in Edinburgh was an option, keep working with his brother-by-law and stay out of the fray. But the idea of resting on his laurels, even after the Ross defeat in the Highlands, held no appeal to Gill. A warrior first, a believer in the English claim to Scotland second, he felt compelled to contribute somewhere other than the tailor shop.

At first, he considered journeying south, joining with the clans there that supported King Edward. They would surely welcome him to knock the false Scottish King from his pedestal.

Then another plan formed in his mind as the barmaid asked if Master Finlay would like another ale.

Master Finlay. That is how most knew him in Edinburgh. Nary a man was left in the Highlands who would know him as Gillivry Ross, and none in the Lowlands might know him as anything other than Gillivry Finlay. Perchance he could put his new identity to better use. Perchance he could spy on the Scots King, or at least the kin of his most devout supporters. Just as he did in Edinburgh, he could come to town with no more than a name, offer his services, and see which way the wind blew across the Scottish soil. If he should provide solid information to the English, to King Longshanks himself even, 'twould put him in a good place once England crushed this false King and his backward Highland followers into the earth.

Slamming his mug on the worn plank counter, he flipped a coin to the barmaid for his drink and made his way back to Finlay's shop. Gillivry needed to thank him and his sister for their hospitality before departing.

Chapter Three: Unsettled

Clan MacCollough, BlackBraes, Southeast of Ullapool

CAITRIN'S DARK BLONDE hair caught on the wind, wild as a lion's mane, and she struggled to tie the kerchief beneath her chin to keep it under control. Sometimes she truly envied those women with long, smooth tresses that obeyed a comb, remained in their braids, and didn't fly out from under a kerchief. Caitrin's hair had never been the coiffure of noble ladies, but more the locks of the lion crests she had seen on English banners when she lived in Wales.

Even her brother's hair, though clipped shorter than hers, behaved as it should. And if it didn't, he had nary a care. A Highlander with a robust head of hair was seen as manly and powerful. For a woman, it was unkempt. She sighed, tucking more of the flyaway tendrils under the dusky brown kerchief as best she could.

Lady Elayne had graciously offered the services of a maid to help Caitrin get her hair under control, but that seem too much for a simple lass like Cait. She was no lady, and the notion of a maid doing her hair bordered on sinful. Truth be told, at times she was grateful for her unladylike hair. She had more than enough troubles with men and their attractions — the last thing she needed was smooth, desirable hair to boot. Looking like a rough peasant had its benefits, at least to Caitrin.

Her concerns of her hair, however, fell to the wayside when she joined her mother out on the narrow stone landing adjacent to the steps that led to the yard. The general bedlam of *BlackBraes* had unnerved her when she arrived with her mother months ago. Now it had become nothing more than a din in the background. This cacophony in the yard, though, was different from the typical sounds of the stronghold, and Caitrin found herself racing outside just like one of the heathens she lived with.

Davina, her mother, leaned over the stone wall, squinting at the man in the yard who clasped Declan MacCollough in a brotherly embrace. She didn't recognize the man and told her daughter as much.

Not that Caitrin had asked. One concern that grew more and more for Davina was Cait's lack of a voice. Having been raised in a convent, then living as maidservants for a minor lord in Wales, Caitrin lived in quiet worlds, ones where women spoke little, if at all. Before the MacCollough keep, her silence was almost unnoticeable, but here, in this rough clan in the Highlands, her daughter wanted to disappear without a voice. And her silence added to her attempts to be a wallflower. Perchance Caitrin hoped her silence would keep her hidden in the shadows of the keep.

As she watched her son celebrate the return of his friend, Davina let her thoughts drift to the stunning lass standing next to her. Davina herself was a beauty; even as an older woman, she received compliments. Compared to her daughter Caitrin, though, every woman paled in Cait's presence. Caitrin's voice may be quiet, but her looks spoke loudly enough to more than compensate. Stunning was an understatement.

With her wild, dark blonde tresses, startling hazel green eyes, and buxom shape, Caitrin was unable to remain the wallflower she desired to be. Before the lass had turned sixteen, Davina and the lord she served had fielded countless offers for the lass's hand. Davina was able to turn down suitors, but she wouldn't be able to reject them much longer. The lass was of an age to wed, and quiet or not, she would have to voice her preference soon, or find herself wed to a man she may not desire. Remaining unwed wasn't an option for the sister of the Laird.

Rumbling voices near her spoke the words "The King" and "King Robert," and Davina gasped. Below the landing, Davina's son, Laird Declan MacCollough, introduced his own statuesque wife to King Robert, who bowed low and kissed her hand in a most gallant manner. No wonder King Robert the Bruce was so beloved, Davina mused. He certainly knew how to play to a crowd!

Declan then led the King up the step and gestured to his mother. She smiled at the Bruce, astonished she was in such a position to have an introduction to King Robert the Bruce himself. Davina stepped to the side, allowing Declan to introduce his sister as well. The lass, per usual, kept silent, only inclining her chiseled face to the Bruce.

The loquacious King, for once, was near speechless, much like every other man upon meeting Caitrin. Even he was not immune to her myriad charms. Robert reluctantly tore his soft brown eyes away from Caitrin to Declan.

"Were I no' already married," he intoned to his friend, "I would wed the lass here and now. 'Tis your sister, ye say?"

Declan's grin spoke his opinion of such a grand idea to the King. "Aye, your Grace. My long-lost sister."

King Robert flicked his eyes back to the lass. She stood with her gaze averted, as if trying to shrink away — something she would never be able to do successfully, the King thought with conviction. Such beauty would always shine through, no matter how much she tried to hide behind rough, dull clothing. In all of his travels, of countless women he'd met, bedded, and even wed, none held a candle close to the MacCollough lass.

"Come, Declan, let us rest our weary souls by the hearth and drink ale to celebrate my return!" the King announced, clapping his hand on Declan's back as he reluctantly made his way past the strikingly beautiful lass. Walking into the keep, he leaned in close to Declan's ear. "We shall have a conversation about your dear sister."

Declan's chest clenched at the King's words. He glanced over his shoulder at his bonnie sister who shrunk as best she could behind their mother. He understood and dreaded what the King intimated — strong clan alliances had been made by marriage with less-attractive women.

And he feared what his mother would say when he told her what the King insinuated. Unlike his sister, his mother had nary a qualm speaking her mind. Nor did his wife, unfortunately, and he didn't want to have this conversation with either one of them. Declan considered his best course of action was to keep his mouth shut.

***

In her always concerted efforts to make herself less obvious, to attract as little attention to her comeliness as possible, Caitrin wrapped a heavy plaid of muted reds and greens around her shoulders and made her way to the stables. 'Twas late in the morning, and Caitrin found peace in working alongside the milkmaids. She hoped that, with the excitement, the maids were slow to their chores and her own beloved cow, Nettie, had not yet been milked.

The dim light of morning filtered through exposed spaces in the wood beams of the barn, and tiny motes of dust and hay danced in the air like fairy folk. A gentle lowing carried from the rear of the barn, and she found Nettie there, a flimsy stalk of hay sprouting from her thick lips as she contentedly chewed her cud.

Caitrin caressed the beast's thick coppery fur, the lowing sounds of the beast vibrating against her fingertips. She often wished her life could be as uncomplicated as Nettie's.

As of late, Caitrin had come to enjoy the solitude of the barn much more than the loud chatter of the keep or the bailey. With the arrival of Robert the Bruce, that uproar only increased, becoming achingly unbearable. She was a quiet woman, and many of the MacColloughs assumed her to be either rude or simple. Truly, Caitrin didn't know which was worse. All she knew was she was grateful for the barn's quiet asylum.

Her brother tried so hard to include her in the running of the keep. The joy Declan exuded at the appearance of Caitrin and her mother runneth over, to be sure. Only, Caitrin was unaccustomed to such attentions. Daily he checked on her, asked how she fared, inquired if she needed anything. Even the sanctity of her own humble chambers was not immune from the invasions of her long-lost brother.

And if 'twere not Declan, then his wife, Elayne, intruded on her privacy on a regular basis. Caitrin had to forgive the poor woman, though. Lady Elayne had been raised without a mother or siblings and was sent to a strange man for an arranged marriage, all of which must have been difficult.

Yet the tall, striking woman handled it with aplomb. Caitrin could easily understand Elayne's loneliness as a child, having experienced similar feelings herself. She tried to endure the Lady's incessant talking, honestly she did, and Cait's own quiet nature encouraged Elayne to fill the silences with banal conversations. In truth, after months in her brother's keep, Caitrin found herself making excuses or outright hiding from the Lady of *BlackBraes*.

She wasn't proud of her behavior toward her brother's wife. Caitrin should be pleased at being reunited with family, of finally having a home of her own, of having siblings. 'Twas what she thought she wanted after years of lonely childhood. Instead, she saw the way the men and women of the keep stared at her, the strange, silent sister of the chieftain. Unlike Elayne, Caitrin didn't welcome attentiveness. And she ran away from those stares as often as she could.

Keeping herself busy with chores around the stronghold helped with that endeavor. She figured if she were hard at work, the chances of someone trying to engage her in idle conversation diminished. And she was accustomed to rough chores — first at the convent, then at the Welsh castle — Cait found peace in the solitude of work.

Entering the barn, she was delighted to find the cow needed her attentions. Caitrin kicked the crude stool close to the cow and grabbed a dented metal bucket from the corner. Skirts lifted, she settled comfortably on her seat and unwrapped her plaid from her shoulders before putting her fingers to work. The barn was warm, much warmer than she expected for early spring. The cold had clutched the Highlands in a fierce grip, and she rather hoped that the old wives' belief of a spring that entered like the lion would depart like the lamb held true. She feared 'twould be years before she grew accustomed to the frigid, snowy winters of Northern Scotland.

Huffing her breath into her cupped palms to warm them, Caitrin leaned her clear forehead against the cow's soft fluffiness. It was like resting upon a downy blanked, a breathing, living blanket. Sighing with relief, she reached to the teats of the cow's bulging udder, and setting the bucket in the line of fire, deftly squeezed and released, allowing frothy milk to fill the bucket.

***

So engrossed as she was in her ministrations to the agreeable cow, Caitrin failed to hear anyone enter the barn. Her bright, intense eyes were closed as her nimble fingers knew what to do without her guidance. She appeared to be sleeping against the side of the cow, her own breath rising and falling in steady cadence to the cow's breath and the pace of the milking.

Torin preferred solitude nearly as much as Caitrin did, and he was more than welcome into her place of peaceful reverie. When the door squeaked open, pale shafts of light permeated the dim interior, catching on hay and dust motes that danced in the rays. Cait didn't even lift her eyes at his entrance. Torin made sure to secure the barn door well, in hopes that no one else would come investigate. Usually found in the stables or the barn at the back, Torin saw the animals as an escape from the world that had so harshly chewed him up and spit him out. In this way, he and Caitrin were of one mind. Though he didn't know it, they both shared the same disdain for the chaos at the keep.

Surprisingly light on his toes for such a large man, Torin moved silently and rarely spoke while in the barn, if he spoke at all. Caitrin and Torin often spent time together, each in their own quiet space among the animals, their common refuge. And the longer Caitrin lived at *BlackBraes*, the more he found her finding a chore that would bring her to the barn. In the short time they encountered each other, they shared nary a word. At best, they each gave a slight nod in welcome, and that was it.

Torin noticed Caitrin resting against the cow in the darkened corner, her hands working seemingly without thought. She was like an animal herself, a wild horse, or a lion perhaps — with her own mane of dark blonde hair that blended into the cow. The stress that often lined her face amid the crowds of the MacCollough clan smoothed, and Torin appreciated the beautiful serenity that effused her whenever he came upon her in the barn.

Presently, her eyes were closed, so he left her with the cow and pulled out his tools to brush down the steeds and clean their hooves for the day. The tinkling sound of his tools did little to interrupt her, and she didn't move from her place on the stool.

Too soon, the cow had no more milk to give. The remaining cows had already been milked, and other than patting several goats in a narrow pen, there was naught else to occupy her in the barn. Wrapping her plaid around her shoulders, she sighed with weighted exaggeration, her shoulders sloping in defeat. 'Twas time to take the milk inside, which meant returning to the bustling noise of the keep.

Caitrin kept her eyes on the barn animals as she approached the large double doors, ignoring Torin as she passed by. The giant man didn't raise his head but spoke in a soft tone as she walked past.

"Do no' fret such, lassie. Ye can escape to the animals later today. I'm sure a horse or two would appreciate your fine ministrations with a brush afore the day's end."

Caitrin paused, her back to the rough man. 'Twas her desire to escape the daily engagements at the keep so obvious? She feared that her brother or good-sister would also notice and try to involve her in activities at the keep. Her breath caught at the prospect of more noise, more people. A shudder coursed through her body. She wondered if Torin noticed her shivers.

"We'll find a way to keep ye coming to the barn, Cait. We think alike, I believe. No better place to find yourself than in a barn with animals who make only quiet demands."

'Twas as though the man could read her mind. Caitrin turned slightly and curtsied to the giant, noting how he managed his immense size in such a cramped space and his kind, astute words. Marching from the barn, she readied herself for the louder, less serene conditions of *BlackBraes*.

Chapter Four: When the Stables are Not Quiet

CAITRIN PICKED HER way across the mushy yard, milk pail in hand. While the milk needed to be put in the buttery as soon as she entered the kitchens, dread built inside her with each step. The chaos of the MacCollough keep, spilling out into the yard, was unnerving — the constant talking, drinking, and cheering tried her patience.

That noise had increased in tone and timber with the arrival of the Bruce. The high spirits of men at the *BlackBraes* meant more drinking, more carousing. The hall teemed with men eating, snoring, and emitting every foul manner of bodily sounds. Even when ensconced in her chambers on the upper floor, the cacophony drifted up through the windows and through the solid stone floor, taunting her as she tried to read, pray, and sleep.

More alarming was the way the King's intense brown eyes followed her movements whenever she was in the keep. Try as she may to hide, the King barred no shame in his appreciation of her. Caitrin had seen that look on many a man's face, a look of eagerness and leering grins, one that bespoke a lascivious desire to bed her, willing or no. The Bruce's sharp and assessing gaze left no question, neither did the words she overheard the King speak to Declan. He may want her himself, but as a married man, and a King who needed allies, the highborn sister of one of his strongest laird's was akin to a gift from God.

She had heard rumors of what happened to young daughters of highborn men — wedding daughters off for political or financial reasons was a well-known and accepted practice, recognized even by sheltered lassies like Caitrin. She understood King Robert the Bruce may want to leverage her position, her status, and should she dare say her virginity, to make the most powerful alliance he could. Her mother and Declan would be powerless to stop his Highness from pressing his advantage.

Her eyes searched the yard as she closed in on the keep, trying to avoid the King of Scotland. She shuddered at her dark thoughts as she entered the kitchens, where even the warmth of the hearth and the smell of fresh oatcakes couldn't chase away the icy thoughts – that her life, one she had lived so simply, so quietly, and may soon no longer be her own. Hiding in the kitchens, hiding from the King himself, seemed her best option. Caitrin could only hope the King forgot about her as he focused on raising his army.

Declan MacCollough and his friend the King of Scotland passed several days together, apprising the Bruce of local events, evaluating the loyalties of the Scottish clans, and accepting fealty of the Highland clansmen gathered at *BlackBraes*.

The Bruce had been forthright in sharing his concerns and needs as King, permitting Declan latitude as his second in command in the Highlands, to rally the clans. Robert had learned the English wolves had kidnapped his wife and daughter — Declan and his men had the unfortunate job of informing him shortly after his arrival that Aymer De Valence, the Earl of Pembroke, had sent a garrison to capture them and most of his family, killing three of his four brothers. Elizabeth and his daughter Marjorie were imprisoned at Lancercost Priory, under King Edward directly. That knowledge made Robert cringe. The Bruce needed to gain control of his country, not just for his men or his crown, but for his wife and child. King Robert confided as much to his friend and ally, Declan.

Many chieftains had sent emissaries to MacCollough keep, awaiting news and directions. While with Declan, the Bruce also evaluated which clans elected to side on the English cause, noting their absence at his councils. Declan admitted that many of the lowland clans saw themselves as nothing more than extensions of the English, so their loyalties were suspect, regardless. Several of the Highland clans appeared to cleave to the English, which surprised and angered Declan and his liege.

Aye, though absent for many months, trying to let the animosity over Comyn's death disperse, the Bruce hadn't truly believed that the clans would turn against him — particularly the Dalziels of Lanarkshire. Their defection to the English wounded the Bruce to his core. These were his friends, his allies, his kinsmen. And now that he wore the crown, once Scotland was settled, he would have to have them tried for treason, a prospect that made his chest ache.

The need to rally the clans and head south — most likely to Douglas land to establish a stronghold closer to the English border, twisted in King Robert's mind, and trepidation overwhelmed him at having to leave the sanctuary of his closest allies. Some days his chest clenched so fiercely he feared he would stop breathing completely.

He also dreaded the news he must break to MacCollough — that the King wanted his close advisers, MacCollough included, to make that journey with him. And another, more harrowing request pulled at Robert's mind, a request that MacCollough would surely find offensive and lead to a harsh exchange of words. The plan forming in his mind would be so appalling to Declan, 'twould seem like a betrayal. The King sighed inwardly at the prospect.

In the meantime, Robert the Bruce spent his days with Declan and several other men, hunting the last of the winter rabbits in the snowy foothills near the MacCollough stronghold, losing himself in the simple joys of the hunt. Chilled air, creating puffs of breath as they rambled across the frosty hills, invigorated them. The King's mood changed dramatically for the better after his arrow felled a second rabbit, surely making for fresh rabbit stew this eve.

When they returned, the yard had transformed into a dusky rainbow of grays, greens, blues, and reds. The clashing of steel and cheering of Highland men and women welcomed the Laird and his King. MacCollough and the Bruce nudged their horses to the loose ring of kinsmen watching the events in the mud.

The giant was unmistakable. With dark russet hair that flowed from his head to his face and neck, and his thickly muscled arms and chest, Torin wore only a green plaid belted around his waist. A film of sweat coated his heaving chest as he moved around the muddy circle. As it stood in the MacCollough clan, he was oft compared to a bear for his size and sheer amount of hair. Torin wielded his claymore against the poor Sinclair man who, in a moment of insanity Declan could only guess, challenged Torin. If the man were fortunate, he would leave the fight with naught more than serious bruises and abrasions for his audacity. If he were not . . .

To watch the mock battle was to see the story of David and Goliath unfold, only without the outcome in David's favor. Larger, more competent men than the Sinclair had challenged Torin, only to receive busted noses and broken bones for their efforts. Surely Torin would kill the lad with the claymore — already the Sinclair was tiring, moving slowly with his own broadsword often dragging in the mud — but 'twas not Torin's way. Once the giant saw his opponent tiring, he would toss the sword to the side and finish the fight with his fists. That way he would only injure his Highland kin, not kill him.

That moment, Marcus Sinclair, the Sinclair Laird's youngest brother, hardly able to lift his steel to his chest, missed his thrust, and Torin knocked the sword from the man's hands with a swift twist of his wrist. Fearful shock overcame Sinclair. His mouth dropped open as he stared upward at the giant coming down on him. With one clean hook to Sinclair's jaw, Torin laid the man low. The crowd of men, Laird Asper Sinclair and his cocky younger brother John included, winced loudly at the punch.

Declan, too, cringed noticeably at the hit the man took. Declan was too familiar with the pain and impact of one of Torin's hammer-like punches, having been on the receiving end of them more than once. The Sinclair was unconscious in the mud, but alive. He would awake soon with his health intact, but nary his pride. And 'twould be a while before another misguided kinsman would challenge Torin. Declan grinned at his muddy man-at-arms and received a twinkle of white from under Torin's beard in return.

A raucous, celebratory dinner was too much for Caitrin to tolerate, even with the promise of fresh rabbit stew. Highlanders, including many from the Sinclair clan who lost coin betting against Torin in the fight, came up to the giant to clasp his arm with pride, and drink flowed like a river through the main hall. Idle conversation held no interest, even as Lady Elayne tried earnestly to engage Caitrin in topics the lass might find interesting. Caitrin admired the Lady of the keep. Ever one to know her mind and let everyone else know it, she was tall, composed, and able to manage the pandemonium of the clan and its present guests. How could one not be impressed?

But the good lady could see that Caitrin was not interested in mundane conversation, her mind elsewhere as her delicate fingers picked at the threads of her skirts.

"Are ye well, Cait?" Elayne probed gently. The bonny lass nodded, silent as always.

"Ye seem to be more quiet than usual. Can ye share with me why?"

Caitrin shifted her eyes around the room, eyes that became a kaleidoscope of colors as her gaze roamed. Elayne understood her meaning.

"Too many people, aye?" She gave Caitrin a small smile and was rewarded with Caitrin gifting Elayne a neat showing of teeth. While that was the partial truth, Caitrin didn't want to share her concerns regarding the King with Elayne. The woman didn't need to carry that weight, and Caitrin had no certainties regarding the King's intentions anyway.

"The men, especially, can be too much. I ken ye. 'Twould be easier if they took their raucous behavior out o'doors."

Elayne's own silver gaze wandered around the room, aware of how easy 'twould be to lose one's voice in such a ruckus. Lady Elayne was renowned for her outspoken ways, and even she found it difficult to make herself heard at times. Plus, the added King's men created an even more tumultuous scene. She pursed her lips.

"Would ye like to escape from the din?" Elayne's smile widened, reaching her fierce silver eyes.

Caitrin marveled at how composed the Lady was amid the chaos. Her own slender fingers played nervously along the seam of her kirtle as she inclined her head. Lady Elayne, for all her forceful ways, truly had a noble spirit. None deserved to rule a clan more than she.

"Aye, please, milady. 'Twould be a grand relief." Her voice was so low that Elayne strained to hear. But she had known what the lass's answer would be when she asked.

Leaning forward, Elayne gently kissed both of the lass's fair cheeks and dismissed her with a wave of her hand.

***

Caitrin at first disappeared in the direction of the dark, cold steps that led to her chambers, but the caterwauling of the celebratory kinsmen echoed off the limestone. Realizing that the din would continue up to her chamber and disturb any peaceful endeavors she may attempt, Caitrin spun on her toe, venturing through the kitchens and out to the yard.

Rather than attending the animals in the barn, she hurried past the rear door to the front stables, hoping the soft neighs and soothing breaths of the horses would help her find the serenity she desired.

The front stable doors were snuggly secured — the stable lads made sure to keep the horses safe at Torin's direction, especially since the Bruce's horse dwelt within. She pushed open a heavy, wooden door, its high-pitched creak the only sound breaking the solitude.

Hay and horsehair hung in the thickly scented air which was warmed by the beasts. She inhaled, breathing in the peaceful surrounding and the heady aroma and exhaling the turmoil of the hall. Calmed already, she lit a low rush light from her tallow candle to illuminate the stalls, the pale light forming a glowing circle about her.

Lady Elayne's white mare nickered at Caitrin. Reaching for the horse, she cupped its velvety muzzle in the palm of her hand. The horse shook her mane lightly, and it shimmered in the incandescent light. Elayne was truly fortunate in such a creature — the mare was vision from a dream. How could one fret in the presence of such magnificent beasts?

A squeaking behind her announced another evening visitor to the stables, Torin most likely, Caitrin assumed. Knowing that the behemoth of a man would leave her to her thoughts and commit to his own business, Caitrin ignored the sounds, sweeping her fingers along the unyielding jaw of the mare that nuzzled her other hand.

"Weel, 'tis my lucky day. A ready woman, here in the stables, waiting for me."

Caitrin whirled around, eyes wide with fear and contempt, to face a drunken Highlander with a leering expression and a randy hand upon the front of his kilt. Her eyes moved from his hand to his face, and after a moment of surprise, she feinted to her right in a meager attempt to flee. Caitrin was no stranger to what men wanted when well in their cups.

The drunken Scot was not about to lose his bounty and matched her movement by shifting left, grasping her upper arm. He stumbled onto her as he did so, his slobber and rotten breath overwhelming her senses. Choking and coughing, she managed a surprising fit of strength to push the man away. Frantic, she rushed past him toward the stable door, only to have a dirty hand grasp the hem of her kirtle, yanking her off her feet. She squealed and floundered into the hay stacked at the base of the mare's stall, losing her plaid wrap in the darkness.

The horses, particularly the affronted mare, noted the discontent in the stables and kicked up in their stalls, their stomping and neighing rising to match the noise of the main hall. Their panic only added to Caitrin's as the man lurched to where she lay askew.

Not bothering with any further attempt at puffing speeches, he flipped up his kilt, knelt above her, and clutched at her kirtle, ripping the fabric to her waist so her left breast sprung free. Hot tears came unbidden, and she screamed, punching her fists at the man's chest and face. She wasn't aware her voice could be so loud.

A thunderous explosion splintered the stable door off its hinges, surprising the man so he fell back on his heels. As his drunken gaze tried to comprehend the invasion, a giant hand landed on the drunken Scot's neck, lifting him into the air. Once his feet dangled above her, Caitrin scrambled backward to the shadowy corner of the horse stalls, covering her breast with the tatters of her gown. She cowered against the wall and watched Torin thrash the Scot like a possessed beast. Caitrin squinted, trying to watch and avert her gaze at the same time.

Torin's bushy beard and wild hair gave him the appearance of an enraged bear, and his actions furthered that image. A deep roar rose from Torin's chest, a sound of pure fury at the man's misplaced aggressions. He threw the man against the remnants of the stable door, where he made solid contact and slid to the ground in a broken heap. Torin followed with a meaty fist to the man's face, bloodying his nose and knocking him senseless. Then, picking up the unconscious man, Torin discarded him outside in the damp grass, leaving him to live or die as he was wont. Torin didn't care.

As soon as the man was disposed of, Torin shifted his attentions to Caitrin, who shrunk even lower into the corner of the stalls. Slipping the fur wrap off his shoulders, he placed it gently over Caitrin, making faint shushing sounds as he did so, like he was trying to calm a skittish horse. His estimation of Caitrin was not far off. The large animals in the stalls stilled before the lass did.

At first, she tried to slide back, away from his reach, but once he covered her modestly with his fur wrap and moved no closer, Caitrin's panic subsided. Her dainty hand wiped tears from her cheeks, and Torin felt another stab of anger, that this drunken Scot distressed Caitrin, and would have done worse had he not arrived in time. She was far too tender of a soul to be subjected to the rank behavior of soiled, sotted men.

He crouched by her feet, trying to calm her with his presence without frightening her further. Her breathing slowed and the terror in her fair face abated, Torin's fury at the Scot along with it.

"Are ye well, lassie?" he inquired in a whispery tone.

Caitrin nodded, unable to find her voice.

"Did he hurt ye, lassie? Do we need to find your brother?"

Her eyes widened, and she shook her head desperately.

"Nay," she begged, her voice fragile and shaking. "The man did no' injure me a'tall. I am well, truly."

'Twas the most Torin heard the lass speak in the time he'd seen her in the barn. To be honest, in all the time she had been at *BlackBraes*. Amusement flitted across his face at her reaction, the tiny peek of white amid his russet beard the lone evidence of his smile.

"Do I need to finish wi' him?" Torin flicked his head at the door. Caitrin lifted her milky white hand to her neck fretfully.

"Nay! The man has suffered enough, I think. He was unable to, um, complete his efforts," she explained in a quivering tone.

At this, Torin had to bite back a laugh. Innocence radiated from the lass brighter than light from the sun, and her larger concern was that the man who attacked her suffered no more. Torin cleared his throat and held out a calloused hand.

"Can I help ye to your feet, Cait? I dare say ye may want to return to your chambers and fix your gown?" Torin kept his eyes on hers in a chaste gesture.

Caitrin's wavy blonde hair fell from her kerchief as she moved her gaze to her chest, as though she could see the ripped gown beneath the fur. Resigned to returning to the keep after so short a refuge in the stables, she sighed and took his hand.

'Twas the first time they had touched. Torin nearly pulled his hand back from her grasp, as though her very skin burned him. A streak of heated lightening shot from his hand to his chest, making his heart skip a beat, and a moment of surprise overtook him. Why did the timid lass have such an effect on him?

Fortunately, she didn't seem to notice, busy as she was brushing hay from her skirts. After she was steady on her feet, she adjusted her gown and shifted the fur wrap around her shoulders. The fur was large enough to cover her nearly to her hips, and the sense of safety and security she had sought in the stables returned. At the stable door, she hesitated. Torin placed a light hand on her back, grounding her.

"Dinna fret, lassie. I will escort ye to your chambers. None will accost ye while I am here."

Caitrin's hazel green gaze drifted from his legs thick as tree trunks, to his broad chest, to his bear-like shoulders and determined face. Aye, she had to agree. No man would approach her with the warrior Torin by her side.

"Thank ye," she whispered.

He held her arm, walked her to the keep and up to the sanctuary of her chambers. Only when he heard the bolt slide into place did he leave the main house to clean up the drunken

Scot and the mess in the stable, attend to the horses, and repair the stable door 'afore anyone came asking, trying to take his mind off the quiet lass who often consumed his thoughts.

***

While Torin escorted Caitrin to her chambers, Robert the Bruce was well into his cups, considering the MacCollough clan's position in the Highlands. Most inhabitants of the keep, and the MacCollough clan in general, were not known for their gentility or placidness. In fact, quite the opposite. Only in the past few months had Declan and Lady Elayne managed to corral the clan into some semblance of respectability. But reckless behaviors died hard, and title of raucous, while better than its previous titles, still clung to the clan.

And that title was exactly what the King of Scotland counted on. His only hope to regain a solid footing as King and defeat the English would be with the wild, devoted Highlanders and their rabid, militant Highland charge. As of yet, few clans had sworn their fealty, and Robert the Bruce feared that he waited too long to return.

Declan MacCollough, though, was not one of those clans. His loyalty to the Bruce was well-known and revered amongst the Highlands. The MacKenzies, MacNallys, MacLeods, Sinclairs, and Grants had sent their representatives, or their Lairds, swearing their loyalty and alliance to the Bruce. The Bruce's advisers assured him that the Camerons, Stewarts, the lowland Fergusons and Douglases, and of course, the MacDonalds, would assuredly follow.

The MacDonald clan worried Robert the most, he had confided earlier to Declan. They had been eternally loyal, their own hatred of the English legendary in the Highlands. Yet, Robert hadn't received a single response, heard any gossip, or received any assurances of their fealty to the Bruce. Where were the MacDonalds? Surely, they should have sent men to meet him at the MacCollough keep already?

These dire thoughts and more plagued the Bruce's mind as he settled into a fur-covered chair before the hearth. The Highland nights, notoriously cool, blew a frigid wind this eve, and even the blazing fire and warm mead could not stop the shivers upon his spine.

The Highland men had sought either their beds or the beds of some fair lasses, and the King of Scotland claimed the hall for his brooding. The muffled sound of steps on the rushes interrupted his reverie, and he was not surprised to see Declan slump into a chair across from him, stout mug in hand.

Sipping his own spiced mead, Declan waited as the moment in front of the fire spun out. Then he turned his astute, gold gaze to his liege lord.

"What ails ye, your Grace?" The Laird MacCollough may have been no more than a servant of the King's, but he believed himself a close enough adviser, and friend, to speak plainly.

Robert appreciated the inquiry, his soft brown eyes squinting at MacCollough.

"Several worries weigh upon my shoulders," Robert began, his jaw set in a firm line. "I ken ye as my ally, 'tis certain. And ye and my kin have assured me the clans will flock to my banner." He paused to sip his chalice, gathering his words.

"Yet, I fear they will no' take the charge. What shall I do if they clans dinna follow me?"

Declan opened his mouth to speak, but Robert lifted his hand to silence him.

"And then there are rumors that the English armies are settling near the border. Already de Valence had command of the English in the south. I have nay doubt that Edward will soon join him, once the pig learns I have returned. And we shall need to make our way south. We can set our armies with the Fergusons, or better the Douglases, I am sure. But —" he paused, inhaling in an aggrieved manner, "that means I have several requests I must ask of ye."

Declan waited. He'd known the King would require him to join the Highland armies, lead them south, and rout the vile Edward and his cronies. As practical as Lady Elayne may be, 'twas a conversation with Elayne he was dreading. But several requests? Declan's curiosity was piqued.

"I must knight several of the men who are here, those who will traverse south with us. Ye have men who are ready to march under my banner?"

Declan nodded at Robert, mentally creating a list of men, and waited for Robert's other requests. They continued drinking, the mead flowing freely, and their thoughts were tinged by drink.

"And I may need your sister."

Had Declan been sipping at his mead, he would have spit it out into the fire. As it was, he sobered immediately. *The King wanted his sister? His Highness was already wed. Did he want her as a mistress?* A treasonous anger toward the Bruce flared in Declan's chest and boiled his mind, and he had to tamp it down forcibly. Otherwise, he feared he would commit a full act of sedition on a man he considered his liege lord and friend.

Caitrin was the focus of many men — that was well-known. The interest in the mysterious sister of Declan MacCollough, it seemed, had extended all the way to the King of Scotland.

So dissimilar from her bold brother or his willful wife, the reticent, golden lass was considered an enigma among those at *BlackBraes*. And while she was always treated courteously, even liked by the kitchen maids, she remained a mystery, even to her brother.

Fortunately, the King hastily continued. "'Tis nay a surety, but to solidify my alliances with some of the clans, I may have to offer up a valuable prize. Your sister is the highest one I have at my disposal."

Declan choked on the words. *At his disposal?* As though his sister were naught more than coin to be given to any man who wanted it? Bile collected at the back of his throat, and once again, he worried he may commit an act of treason.

"Your Grace," Declan began most respectfully, trying to keep his ire hidden. "I canna in good conscious promise ye that. Our mother will be of a mind regarding her daughter's future. I have only had her in my household for half a year. And ye may have noted the lass's nature. She was raised, for much of her life, in a convent before she and my mam left to work for a nobleman. Caitrin is of a reticent nature and may feel a calling for the holy orders."

The Bruce's eyes darkened in a way that frightened Declan to his core, and he was not a man who frightened easily. Declan may be the chieftain of his clan, but this was his King, and to refuse his request, his orders, was a form of treason.

Contrite, he dipped his head to the King. "My apologies, your Grace. I mean no offense."

The Bruce sighed heavily, placing his royal hand on Declan's arm. "I dinna ask this lightly, Declan," he admitted, his mead-tinged breath hot on Declan's face. "I willna ask it unless I have to, absolutely have to. But as of yet, she is unwed. Unless that situation should change soon, she will become a bartering chip."

Pausing to sip from his chalice once more, the Bruce cut his eyes to Declan. "Your wife was an arranged marriage, and I dinna see either of ye complaining."

"Ye dinna ken my wife," Declan said mostly under his breath, but the Bruce still heard it. "She had more of a choice, the option to reject me if she desired. And I dinna believe the Lady Elayne will take to this form of barter. She is, um, forward-thinking and quite brash for a lady, aye?"

The King chuckled, having heard tales of Lady Elayne's viperous tongue. "But ye will keep my needs in mind, will ye now?"

The weight of the King's words lay on Declan's shoulder, who didn't fail to miss the suggestion put forth. *Unless that situation should change . . . Was his sister interested in wedding at all? Did that include a bride of Christ as a nun? Damn this cryptic man!*

Declan nodded respectfully at the Bruce, trying to keep an open mind. The King was in a difficult place, to be sure. The MacCollough needed that reminder to stay at the front of his thoughts at all times.

And who knew what the future would hold? Perchance his sister had a love interest that could soon become a husband, and then any obligation to his liege lord would be moot. Declan could only hope. He assuredly didn't want to tell his wife of the King's intentions, so he would keep this conversation about his sister to himself. *More secrets*, Declan lamented. For the first time in their history, a formidable unease settled over him as he climbed into bed with his wife.

Chapter Five: What Happens When We Eavesdrop

CAITRIN RESTED ON her bed after a busy day feeding and cleaning up after the King's Highlanders. Her feet ached from running fore and aft throughout the day. The muscles in her arms screamed from drawing water from the well, kneading loaves of brown bread, and carrying platter after platter laden with food out to the hall.

Then, after each round of cooking, they needed to scrub the kitchens and begin again. The housemaids had not even started on scrubbing the great hall, and Caitrin didn't envy them when they did. All her work at the nunnery and then at the Welsh lord's house never amounted to half of what she did over the course of the last twelve hours at her brother's keep. But she was one to look for silver linings, and the busy work helped her forget the wretched events in the barn and the ominous words of the King.

More clans started to arrive during the day, and while most set up camp in the outer yard and even into the thawing glens, the sheer number of men was daunting, which was undoubtedly welcome news for the King. Declan actually caught the man smiling more than a few times, Robert's spirits soaring as more men arrived. Several men even brought their women, which was fortunate. The maids needed the help in the kitchens. Most men tarried in the yard, eating over campfires in the damp air — parritch, dried fish, or small animals they hunted in the grasses or the slender copse of trees. A goodish number, though, traipsed through the hall, swearing fealty to King Robert, awaiting tasks, standing with their chieftains, and they needed to be fed.

Another silver lining — hiding in the kitchens kept her far from ogling Highland Scots parading about the grounds. Few men ventured into the kitchens, seeing it as a place for women. Other than a few young squires, growing lads who seemed to eat their weight in oats daily, the only men Caitrin saw in the kitchens that day were her brother and Kaleigh's husband, Duncan. They ducked into the kitchens for one reason, to check on their own women and steal a kiss, or something a bit more suggestive inside the buttery.

The girls, Caitrin included, giggled every time a couple snuck away, then hid their giggles under serious faces when they reappeared. Caitrin relished laughing with the lassies. They considered each couple's actions the height of romance, a romance many didn't have.

After the kitchens were wiped clean and ready for the havoc of the next day, Caitrin said her fare-the-wells to the other kitchen maids. As she walked to the dark stairway, she took a moment to gaze longingly at the heavy wooden hall doors, which were propped open and invited her outside to the barn to find moment of solitude with the animals. But she was just too worn. Her kirtle was damp and stained, wisps of her hair clung to her sweaty forehead, and her chamber called her name. She flopped onto her bed, fully dressed, sighing with relief. Sleep would come quickly, she was certain.

But after a few moments in the relaxing comfort of her bed, trying to shut out the noises from the hall and yard below, she rubbed her eyes, huffed, and rolled off the bed to her water table. One of the nicer items in her chamber, the table was a rich walnut polished to a high shine. 'Twas the most lovely luxuries she'd ever had at her disposal. A decorated wooden bowl sat atop the table next to a glass pitcher full of scented water topped with a few leaves and flower petals. She ran her fingers over the face towel, nothing more than a clean cloth, that lay folded at the table's edge, waiting for use.

Next to the table, a rich woolen tapestry hung over the narrow window of her room, keeping most of the cooler air outside her chambers. But after feeling locked inside for most of the day, Caitrin craved the fresh air. She fashioned the tapestry to the side, exposing the evening air and the men traipsing around in the yard. Her view included the barn and stables, plus a giant collection of tents under a vast expanse of night that covered the land like a dark blanket. At least she could admire her beloved barn from afar.

Keeping the window open, she reached for the pitcher and poured with a heavy hand, filling the bowl to the brim. She dipped the cloth into the water, wrung it out to avoid any errant drips, then began wiping her hair and face. Resting against the window ledge, she continued to admire the majesty of her brother's land while she wiped herself clean, feeling each layer of kitchen grime peel from her skin.

She rinsed the cloth and worked it beneath the top of her shift, scrubbing at the grit that somehow managed to collect between her breasts. Lifting her face, she again peered out the window, only to have her eyes catch on a lone man standing in the yard, his face upturned to her window.

'Twould be impossible to mistake the man. Caitrin knew only one Highlander that dark and that large. Torin had paused his work in the bailey, oblivious to the surrounding liveliness, rooted in his spot. Caitrin's hand paused in her washing as she was captured under Torin's gaze. Her mind reeled – she pondered why he was watching, *what was he seeing with her at the window?* Flushing with the slow realization that he caught her in an intimate moment of washing, she stiffened even more. She stepped back from the window, pulling on the tapestry to cover the opening, bringing the strangely intimate moment to an end.

Once the tapestry fell into place, Torin blinked several times, trying to gather his wits. Mild disappointment had filled him when he noted Caitrin's absence from the barn, but he figured it more the soundless company she provided and nothing more. 'Twas only when he finished pitching hay into his steed's stall and made his way across the yard did he raise his eyes to her window. He was unsure why he wanted to see her, only 'twas a habit he found himself doing often as of late. A burgeoning sense of hope built inside him that perchance he would see her again this evening.

Then suddenly she was there, her ravishing body silhouetted against the muted light in her room. Torin froze, unable to take his eyes from the vision before him. His gaze followed her as she moved around her room, and when she washed her neck and ran the cloth over her lush breasts, he felt lightheaded. His cock throbbed with unconscious need.

He should have been embarrassed to be caught observing her, spying on her, but he was not. Instead, he hoped she would catch his admiration, to see if she would skitter away as she did from so many people and events. Rather, she remained, even casting her gaze to him. Only after a shared moment did she replace the tapestry, the night suddenly darker and less captivating.

Torin glanced around the yard to see if any other Scotsmen saw him agog like a young lad, or worse, were watching her. To his relief, he saw nothing amiss. Every Highlander seemed too focused on his own concerns to be peeking inside a lassie's window.

That Caitrin hesitated at the window for a moment after catching his gaze perplexed him. He had expected her to retreat with fright and run from the window, not stay and watch him in return. It didn't fit her skittish, timid nature, and his mind wouldn't stop thinking on it.

Or stop thinking about his own reaction. The fire that built inside him as he caught her silhouette was unexpected, and he, too, questioned that lustful response. Years had passed since his wee Janet died after birthing a dead bairn. For so long, the mere thought of his time with Janet caused a painful clenching in his chest, he couldn't even speak of her. She had haunted his dreams, and he had slept fitfully for months afterward. Over the past several months, however, his mind touched on her less. When it did, the memories didn't pain his heart, and her specter no longer visited him in his dreams.

While he didn't want to admit it, those changes began shortly after the arrival of Caitrin and her mother. He could not imagine the two events were related. Especially now that other images filled his nightly visions.

But the more his mind drifted to the fair Caitrin bathing in the window, the more he realized the sadness in his heart had been replaced with longing for his laird's sister.

***

After another long day with the King, meeting Highlanders from across northern landscape of Scotland, corralling the clans into their camps, and making plans to begin moving the army south now that more of the clans had responded to the Bruce's call, all Declan wanted was a quick bath and to fall into bed with his wife.

Robert's mood had changed dramatically over the last day as more clans joined his entourage. Building an army was no small feat after so long an absence, and the King's hope to rally the clans was becoming a reality. His flourishing mood also meant more ale and late nights. Fortunately, King Robert had not resumed his discussion regarding Caitrin, and Declan for one would not remind him. He would keep his mouth shut as long as he needed if it avoided conversations about his sister.

But, 'twas not his wife he found waiting in his room when he entered, much to his chagrin. His mother sat tall and squinting at the door, impatient for his arrival. Davina's mouth pursed into a tight line, her whole face showing her frustration with her son. *She knows,* he thought, and wondered who in the keep had both large ears and a larger mouth.

"Mother," he nodded at her and closed the chamber door, assuring their privacy. "To what do I owe this pleasure?"

The tight line of her lips narrowed impossibly more. "I think ye ken, son."

She let the implication hang and tilted her dark blonde head, so much like his own, waiting for his reply.

"Mother, I dinna think —" he started, then paused. What could he say? How much did she truly know?

"Would ye sell your sister to the highest bidder, like a slave, at the King's behest?"

Aye, she kens everything. How did she find out? He sighed, rubbing his forehead with his fingertips, trying to decide what he could say that would temper his mother's distress.

"'Tis no' like that, mother." The words fell flat. *'Twas like that,* he had to be honest with himself. She summed it up exactly.

"Nay, 'tis like that," she echoed his thoughts. "Do ye nay recall that I was sold to your father for my dowry and position? 'Tis nay an enviable position for anyone, least of all a lass who has no choice. Least of all, *my* lass."

Davina stood, her velvet wrap falling from her shoulders as she moved to Declan. "Son," her voice was so low Declan strained to hear her. "Dinna let your dear, sweet sister be sold to an old man or a violent one. Dinna let her be taken from our home to a strange land."

She grabbed his hands, clutching them to her chest. Her dusky hazel eyes searched his face, imploring.

"Mother, I can nay make that promise —"

He wanted to. He wanted to promise he would be the protector for her and his sister that his father never was, but he had a fealty to the King. Anything less was treason.

"If ye canna make sure Caitrin will be sold like a common pig, I will have to leave. I will protect her just as I did when she was a bairn in my belly. 'Twill kill my heart," she told him, placing a cool hand on his scruffy jaw.

She loved touching his face, having missed it for so long. But she was willing to miss it again, if forced. Davina had sworn no fealty to the King and would do everything in her limited power to ensure her daughter's safe keeping.

"I will no' be whole, if I must leave ye again. But I will, in a heartbeat, with no second thoughts. And 'twould protect ye as well. If Cait is no' here, then the King canna marry her off."

Declan was speechless. The past six months had passed almost as a dream. 'Twas the life he had always wanted as a lad — his mother, his sister, his wife, his clan. His family. He couldn't permit it to come crashing down now. Davina pulled his hand to her lips, kissing it and placing her hand over the kiss, as though to seal it in place.

"I ken ye will do what ye must, son."

She patted his face once more before grabbing her wrap and slipping past him out the chamber door.

Davina ambled a short way across the dimmed hallway, the flickering torches and waxy candles casting frightening shadows as she moved. Once she heard Declan's chamber door secured, she leaned against the chilly stones, breathing hard. Davina hated confrontation — even years after the harsh treatment by her husband, the former, now deceased Laird MacCollough, she struggled to make her wishes known. Repeatedly, she had to remind herself that her son wasn't his father, that he was a kind man to whom she could bring such grievances.

As for the King, well, she would leave addressing him to her son. Declan, she knew, was a close friend and ally, and an excellent diplomat. Robert would assuredly give Declan his ear.

***

The same ears that had overheard Declan and the King and shared that conversation with Davina also made her way toward Caitrin's chamber. Kaleigh believed the lass should have a choice and not, using Davina's words, be sold to the highest bidder in political hopes of an ally.

Kaleigh wasn't proud of her eavesdropping. But neither was it her fault if Laird Declan and his King spoke loud enough to be heard as she finished sweeping the kitchens for the eve. And if she paused by the entryway to the hall to better make out their words, well, she couldn't be faulted for that. They should have spoken in quieter tones, or in the privacy of the study.

Though she heard their discussion several nights prior, what to do with her knowledge troubled her. 'Twas the King's business, not hers. She was naught more than a kitchen maid in the keep — who was she to comment on his decisions, or share what she had heard?

Her husband, Duncan, noted her face did not alight as it usually did when he greeted her in the kitchens. He accompanied her to the gardens for fresh air and the words spilled from her as a river bursting from a dam. While he recommended perhaps keeping the information to herself (discretion was always the better part of valor, he believed), he told Kaleigh to follow her better sense. Mentally, he promised to share everything he knew with Declan as soon as he had more information to pass along.

And this day, Kaleigh had spent much of it working beside Caitrin, and the conundrum caused her more strife as the hours progressed. Finally, before supper, Davina stepped into the kitchens to help serve the food, and Kaleigh pulled her aside, her kerchiefed head bowed as she spoke the King's words to the woman. Davina would know best what to do. And then the weight of it 'twould no longer be on Kaleigh's shoulders.

Kaleigh rounded the steps at the top and found Davina crouched against the wall of the hallway, looking as though she just had a run-in with the devil himself. Davina caught Kaleigh's light blue gaze and nodded at her. Pushing herself off the wall, Davina joined Kaleigh to make her way down to Caitrin's small, private chamber.

"What shall ye do?" Kaleigh asked.

That Caitrin perhaps wanted to return to the nunnery was no secret with the MacColloughs. Kaleigh feared Caitrin's reaction when she learned she must marry to serve the King's political interests, but at least the lass had options, and a mother willing to protect her fiercely.

"I dinna yet ken," Davina answered honestly. "I dinna ken the lass's mind. If she yet even has a love interest. At best, perchance I could squire her away to the convent 'afore the King can arrange a match."

"Could no' the King just call her back? Force her into marriage?" Kaleigh continued, cringing at her own suggestion.

Davina shuddered at the notion of her daughter forced into marriage with a man, one probably several scores older. Her own wedded history with the previous Laird MacCollough was slowly healing wound, one that still ached when she thought on it. She would do everything in her power to prevent that same wound in her daughter.

"As far as I ken, the Church still holds sway over the lives of men, which includes kings." Davina made a huffing sound as they neared Caitrin's door. "'Twould be far easier if the lass were just wed already."

Once they reached Caitrin's door, they faced each other again, then Davina raised her hand and knocked at the door. Her daughter swung the door wide, surprised at her late-night visitors. Her wild, blonde hair was unkempt from the quick wash, and the dusky sleeping shift hung from her lean frame.

"Mother!" she exclaimed. "Kaleigh? Why are ye here so late? I am to bed . . ." Her voice trailed off as Davina pushed past her into the room, dragging Kaleigh with her.

"We must converse, my lassie," her mother began, her tone sharp.

"Mother, what's amiss?" Her eyes shifted from a nervous Kaleigh to her mother.

"Ye must pack. Tonight. We can nay tell your brother, or 'twill be akin to treason. I will no' put him in such a position with his friend and liege lord. But I will no' have ye used as barter."

I kenned it, Caitrin thought in a flash, tightening her lips. But how did Kaleigh or her mother know? Was something more decided than just an offhand comment by the King? Horrified at the prospect that a dire decision had come to pass, Caitrin's milky skin went starkly white.

"Barter!" Caitrin's eyebrows flew high on her forehead, her soft voice rising. "Mother, I think ye should sit and tell me all."

Davina sat on the bedstead as Kaleigh settled on the small stool near the window tapestry. The candlelight cast shadows in the deepest corners, and Davina's words made the room seem even more ominous. Davina flicked her gaze to Kaleigh in acknowledgment before speaking.

"She overheard your brother in discourse with the King," Davina let out in a breathy rush. "'Twould seem, though 'tis no' settled yet, that the King has decided to use ye, your hand in marriage, as a bartering chip to form alliances with another clan."

Caitrin grew as fearful as Kaleigh and began pacing the room, wringing her hands into her shift. *'Twas worse than an offhand comment!* Still, something so important couldn't have happened in so short a time, and she expressed so to her mother.

"Oh, mother, nay. My brother has only just reunited with us. He would no' allow the King to do such a thing as ye have described."

The words sounded hollow in her ears. In her deepest heart, she knew what her mother said was true. Fortunes and futures changed in a moment. Davina shook her ashy blonde head, the lines on her face thickening as she kept her soft gaze on her daughter.

"Nay, my dear Cait. Kaleigh heard it clear enough, and 'tis something kings and lords oft do to secure power, as ye well ken. And your brother is the King's man. Should King Robert say ye need to wed, your brother will have to agree, or he could be tried and hung for treason."

This time the word *treason* caused Caitrin's heart to skip a beat. Surely, the good and rightful King of Scotland wouldn't commit to this decision? He wouldn't put Declan in this position to have to marry off his sister for an ally.

But then her mind went to the men in the yard, the desperation of the clans to throw off English shackles once and for all, the need to unite the Highlands and the whole of Scotland, and she was convinced the King also shared in that desperation. And desperate men oft do desperate things.

Caitrin dropped to her mother's feet, resting her head upon her mother's lap. Davina's fingers threaded through her daughter's thick mane without a thought. A plan had already formed as she had watched Caitrin pace the floor.

"But dinna fret, my lassie," Davina told her. "Your mother has a notion of how to undo this mess and keep Declan in the King's good graces."

***

Caitrin's head shot up from her mother's lap, her green eyes as large as serving platters. "What are ye thinking, mother?"

A slight smile pulled at Davina's lips as she stroked Caitrin's achingly beautiful face. For so long, they had only each other. Once they returned to Declan, hope sprouted again in her chest, that Declan and Caitrin would each wed, have babies, and Davina would be surrounded by family and love. Now, with a stabbing pain in her heart, she had to again lose one of her children. This time, 'twas her bairn, her baby girl, and her solution would mean that Caitrin may never wed, never know the joy of children and love herself.

"We will take ye back to the convent. Back to Mother Superior of ColdStream. If we leave right after the evening meal on the morrow, we can travel under the cover of night and be at ColdStream by late afternoon the following day. Kaleigh," Davina tipped her head to the forgotten lass perched on the edge of the stool, "she will ask her husband, Duncan, to accompany us. We will do all this with nary a word to Declan. Ye canna even say goodbye."

Caitrin's hand rose to her elegant throat. The prospect of leaving her mother, of abandoning her long-lost brother, frightened her. The appeal of a convent, perchance taking vows and living in relative quiet, made for a sound decision. But was living apart from her family, committing to Christ, truly what she desired? Had the King and her own brother honestly left her no other choice?

But as much as she wanted to believe in her mother's plan, the convent idea was most likely a stupid one. Though Duncan would accompany them for protection, either the Lady Elayne or Declan would easily and promptly learn of their departure. Duncan would tell their plans to Declan, without question, out of loyalty to his Laird. 'Twas obvious to all that Declan's men were staunchly faithful to him. While Elayne, the willful woman she was, might assist in their plot, 'twas lunacy to think they could keep such subterfuge from her brother, or even worse, King Robert. 'Twould be akin to treachery.

Caitrin struggled to pull away from her mother's embrace. They shared the same eyes, the same gaze, and Davina's heart wrenched as her eyes roved over the face and hair so like her own but so unique unto her beloved daughter. The pain in her heart became the cutting of a knife, and she blinked back tears. *How had it come to this?*

Silent and stoic, Caitrin stood and, keeping her sights on her mother, bolted from the room.

Kaleigh's fretful expression matched Davina's. They rose together, rushing the doorway, only to watch as Caitrin fled down the stone steps in her bare feet and her night shift, looking like a ghost fleeing the darkened hallway.

Tears blurred Caitrin's vision as she ran from the keep. She didn't know where she was going, only that she needed to escape. As a matter of habit, she found her way to the barn door. Her sanctuary, her solace, and lately, it seemed, the lone place where she felt she had a modicum of control in her life.

This strange limbo, first moving around with her mother, then living with her long-lost brother, not being truly accepted anywhere, plagued her. She ached for a home and feared she would never find it. Now, with the possibility of the King selling her off to the highest bidder, she would lose even this home — this brash collection of strangers she had begun to love.

An arid wind stirred, slamming the barn door against the warped wooden planks as she flung it open. Inviting scents of hay and manure wafted out, the familiar odor calming her shaking hands and wildly beating heart. Inhaling the barn air into her chest with a deep breath, she allowed her mind to clear, trying to forget the damning news she'd just received.

A gentle mewing sound arose from the corner of the barn, and she waded through the hay to where several young goats nestled together. One of the older yearlings lifted his head, peering at her with tired, black eyes. Caitrin's heart softened at the contented gaze from the sleepy goat, and she nuzzled his knobby head with her hand, her tears wetting them both.

***

Usually, Torin was able to put the yard sounds out of his hearing when he slept. He would never have a good night's rest if he couldn't tune out the noise. The animals in the barn and the horses in the stables could be loud enough if 'twere a rough night, but the human animals in the yard were much louder. Sleep did not come easily on nights when rowdy clansmen and kin were deep in their cups.

This night, though, 'twas the wind that made sleep elusive. And the loud banging of the barn doors shot him wide awake. He'd had enough trouble with MacKenzies and other clans in the barn, especially trying to have their ways with young women. While some may be willing, others were less so, and anyone in the barn this late would undoubtedly disturb the animals.

Dressed in only a loose pair of braies, Torin raced from his bed and out into the cold, ducking out of habit to avoid smacking his head against the doorway. He would give whoever dared disturbed the MacCollough animals a beating they would never forget.

The trespassers in the barn had not secured the door well, leaving it rattling with the wind. 'Twas that banging that woke him. Hot with ire over having to come out in the nighttime chill, his chest and face burned red. The wind cut immediately when he stepped into the barn, and heat from his anger caused him to burst into a light sweat. Torin paused a moment, allowing his eyes to adjust to the barn's darkness and listening for the intruder. At the rustling sound to his left, he moved on stealth toes in that direction to confront the trespasser.

He drew up short, however, at the image of the familiar blonde woman cuddling a young goat. Caitrin looked up, shrinking from the large, half-naked Highlander who caught her unawares. At first, she panicked at her lack of dress, clutching her shift to hide herself. When she realized ‘twas Torin, she breathed out a relieved rush of air.

"Lassie!" Torin tried to temper his rough voice. The lass was skittish enough as ‘twas, but he could see she had been crying and didn't want to frighten her more. "What are ye doin' here so late in the eve? 'Tis nay safe, aye?" He rolled his dark eyes toward the barn door.

Caitrin could nary forget her perilous encounter with the drunken Scot, but she would not allow that to halt her visits to the only place she felt welcome. She bit her lip, trying to form words the giant man would understand. Tears formed again, and she wiped them away with her sleeve.

Torin's chest hitched at her movement. As she sat with the wee goatie, she resembled an image he would see in the stained glass at a large kirk. Everything that was good and wonderful in the world seemed to shine from her, and that she should be crying bothered him. *What would cause this gentle soul to weep?* Forgetting his own state of undress, he crouched close to her.

"What ails ye, lassie? Sure 'tis no' as bad as all that?"

To his surprise, she nodded her head. Caitrin lifted her teary eyes to his searching gaze. Other than the evening with the drunkard when he escorted her back to the keep, he had never been so intimate with her. She kept herself so shuttered, so remote. He risked taking her dainty hand, the one not cuddling the goat, in his rough grasp and waited for her to speak.

She swallowed several times before the words came forth. "I dinna ken where to start—" she began but caught herself. "'Tis nay your concern, good sir. I should no' have brought ye here with my sounds of distress."

A low chuckle shook his broad chest, and Caitrin had to force herself to look away from his trembling muscles. ‘Twould be inappropriate to be caught admiring his bare skin.

"Lassie, after the other eve, if ye dinna think I should be concerned, then ye dinna ken me verra well. I do no' permit damsels in distress in my barn."

His bright teeth reflected a wee bit of moonlight from the high window slits. *Was he smiling at her?* Unnerved by his presence and at being caught hiding in the barn, she remained silent. How could she possibly share her petty concerns with this mammoth of a man?

"Go on, lassie," his voice was soft with encouragement. "Ye can tell me. I only want to help ye."

And he meant it. A long time had passed since he felt any emotion toward anyone, other than his Laird, and even that was subdued. The most recent feeling he could recall was his distaste when he initially met Lady Elayne, and even those feelings had dissipated. For years, 'twas a chasm, an emptiness that ruled every day of his life.

Until he saw Caitrin ride up with her mother nigh five months ago. When the lassie pulled back her cowl, he was sure his heart stopped. His breathing did stop, and he had to shake himself to regain his wits.

The emotion he felt at that moment had hit him harder than a punch to the gut. Every time he saw the lass since, that same heart-stopping sensation gave him pause. The sudden rush of heat whenever he encountered Caitrin made his chest ache and scorched his mind *and* his groin. 'Twas almost painful after so many years of no feeling. And it seemed disloyal to his Janet who had loved him resolutely. Not to mention Caitrin was a skittish lass, raised in a convent, his laird's sister, and a woman he could never have. *That* fact complicated his desires toward the lassie more than anything else. Now, though, here in this barn, all those emotions came to a head, and all he wanted to do was help her in any way he could.

The warmth of Torin's hand lit Caitrin's skin ablaze, a fire that traversed her arm and made her heart flutter wildly. His dark eyes held only gentle reassurance, and much to her own astonishment, Caitrin found her voice and shared her predicament with the handsome giant.

"I learned this eve that my stay here with my brother may be short," she began. Her eyes remained downcast as she spoke, otherwise she would have noted his own eyes jolted open wide. "The King, he needs allies, aye? I dinna have a mind for fealties, for politics, for kings and power, but Declan, he's a close friend of the King's. I had heard the King hint that he may have need of me, but I pushed any of those thoughts aside. Surely, that wouldn't happen, aye? Then a kitchen maid overheard the King telling my brother that he may need something of value to make these alliances with other clans, and I am a fine bartering chip. The sister of Laird MacCollough would turn a large clan into a fierce ally indeed."

More tears fell from her weeping eyes onto Torin's hand, but he was too stunned to notice. She crumpled into a heap with her sobbing. *Leave? Wed another?* 'Twas only here in the dark serenity of the barn with this fair lass did Torin finally realize what he had tried to suppress for months. Torin had appreciated her reticent behavior because he didn't want the lass to be with anyone other than him. *He* wanted to be with Caitrin. Jealously welled in his chest, and he counted to ten to calm his baser nature.

He began to place his arm around her shoulders in a show of support, then halted, fearing her skittish nature would take over, and she would run from his embrace. Surprisingly, she leaned into the tense brawn of his arm and settled under the pleasant, protective weight that held her.

Her breath hitched as she continued, speaking more than he'd ever heard her say before. "My dear mam wants me to escape to a convent, take my vows, as 'tis something I had oft considered. The quiet and solitude of ColdStream appeals to me, but I would miss my mam and my newly found brother. By the Bride, I am no' sure I want to take the vows. Even worse, I dinna think we would succeed. My brother, or the King, would learn of it 'afore too long. Skilled riders would easily overtake us, and I'd be in the same position as I am now, only with shackles around my ankles to keep me in my place."

Torin kept silent, taking in the gravity of her words. He agreed with the lass — her brother, to say naught of the King, would not permit the lass to escape if she could be used to form an alliance. Her future seemed dire, undoubtedly.

Weeping overcame her completely, and Caitrin slumped into Torin's chest. He stroked her hair and cooed lightly, at a loss of what to say or do. His mind hammered at the problem. *Was there no recourse? Against his laird? The King?* Torin's own chest ached at the bind she was in and at the terrifying realization he may lose this woman he had only just begun to know and care for.

"Tis truly that dire?" Torin tried to minimize the predicament, not believing all she said could be true. "Surely, your brother might step in? Or his wife? God kens, I can no' imagine Lady Elayne no' protesting this. And 'tis nay for certain, aye? He hasn't made the decision to wed ye off yet?"

Caitrin choked back a sob. "Nay. But Elayne is Declan's wife, so while she may complain and storm about, 'twill all be for naught. Unless I am somehow wed or gone 'afore the King could make a match, I will —"

Torin started, sitting up straight. Caitrin all but fell off his lap. She looked up into his darkly haunting face, unable to read the strange expression he wore.

"What did ye just say?" His question was husky.

"Ooch," Caitrin cleared her throat, adjusting her position on the barn floor. "Only that if I were wed, then I could avoid having to wed a stranger."

"Did the King say that? Out loud? To Declan? Are ye positive he said such a thing?"

Torin had heard the King was a man with a good heart, oft too soft a heart, and if he gave voice to an out, Torin believed 'twould behoove her to use it. A terrifying and bold plan formed behind Torin's hooded eyes.

Caitrin's delicate features twisted at his inquiry. What could he mean? She wasn't wed, so the option was moot. *Wasn't it?*

"Aye, why? Why are ye asking? I have no husband, nary a betrothed, so I am the King's to command."

Torin shook his head, little more than a shadow in the dark. Caitrin straightened fully as Torin placed a thick finger under her chin.

"But what if ye weren't? Nay, Cait. The King's heart can be fairer than his mind. He does no' want to use ye unless he must, and only if the opportunity presents itself. He spoke those words to your brother to let him know that he would no' do wrong by his kinsman if he could avoid it."

The heat between them built as Torin spoke. And his next words lit her on fire and frightened her to her very core.

"Ye need to wed, Cait. Soon. Tonight, or tomorrow if possible. And ye canna tell your brother. It must be kept a secret." Torin took a brief pause to gather his own courage and breathed the next words in a rush.

"Ye need to wed me."

Chapter Six: Secret Plans

SHE FELL BACK into the goat's hay pile, as though Torin stabbed her through her belly rather than asked her to wed. He immediately felt an unfamiliar humiliation at his rash words and tried to scale back the shock of his offer.

"Weel, ye dinna need to," he stammered, a quirk he rarely exposed. "Ye can o'course wed the man the King chooses for ye. And he may no' make any arrangement —" At this, the lassie scoffed.

Caitrin knew that King Robert wouldn't pass on the opportunity to form a strong alliance through marriage. He couldn't – he needed those alliances to win Scotland. No matter how hopeful the situation in Scotland, she was akin to a dangling piece of low-lying fruit. Too juicy and inviting as not to be picked. She would be wedded and bedded 'afore springtime was over. That she knew too well, and so did the hulking man before her. He wouldn't have made such an extreme offer otherwise.

"Ye dinna believe that," she told him. Her voice may have been quiet and low, but the flames in her golden eyes burned with an intensity that illuminated the barn. Torin dipped his head. As much as he or her mother may try to hide the truth, she was all-to-familiar with how the world worked. 'Twas an unfortunate fate for most young lasses.

She kept her forceful, blazing gaze on his face, measuring the weight of his words. 'Twould anger the King, if they wed – 'twas no doubting that. But even the King himself admitted that marriage elsewhere was her only escape.

To make the offer worse, Torin was one of the largest, most frightening men she'd ever encountered. And she had traversed over Scotland and into Wales and had seen many men. Her gaze roved over the man as she considered his offer of marriage. The giant of a Scot may be her brother's tacksman and most trusted friend, but his size? And she had seen the giant and her brother fight and spar; he was the only man who could lay the Laird low in seconds. She would be at his mercy.

If she wedded him, she must bed him, and that prospect made her break out in a sweat. Even in the cold air of the barn, droplets rolled down her back and between her breasts. The sheer breadth of his chest was enough to make her swoon. How could she wed such an immense, dangerous man?

Caitrin gulped as realization washed over her. *How could she not?* She had witnessed firsthand his truly gentle nature, how he had cared for and protected her in the past. Her mind flitted to the night he watched her in her window. A man didn't watch a woman like that unless he had affection for her. That was knowledge she wouldn't have if the King selected her future husband.

But more importantly, 'twas a guise they could pull off. They had spent time together in the barn over the past months — Torin was familiar to her. Who could deny that they had come to desire each other? That the decision to wed was one made out of love and not to avoid the King's dictate?

Torin hadn't moved the entire time she regarded him with those shrewd eyes. Her expression never changed, and he kept his gaze centered on her. The offer was a true one. Though he may not want to admit it out loud, he'd wanted her since that first time he saw her in the yard. To wed the lass was a substantial move, a major life decision, but one he was more than willing to make. And as for her skittishness, well, he made a promise to himself as he watched her make up her mind.

While he would wed her this eve or the next, he would hold himself in check, and wait until she was ready before he bedded her. Then he prayed for the patience to follow through with that promise.

Caitrin must have seen something on his face that spoke to her heart, telling her to trust him, that he would wait on her. 'Twas an expression that told her he would care for her and protect her with his life. Because she reached out her hand, cool and ghostly in the barn, and placed it delicately atop his own. She rose up on her knees, so her face was only a finger length from his. Torin held his breath as he waited for her answer.

"Aye, Torin," her voice was barely above a whisper, yet still echoed in the darkness of the barn. "I will wed ye."

And though 'twas not the best reaction — Caitrin would have scrambled away if she could have — Torin pulled her to his bare chest, enclosing her in a tight embrace.

She squeaked at the movement and stiffened at first, unnerved by the closeness of the bare-skinned giant who smelled of earth, hay, and something unbearably male. His furred skin pressed against her cheek, and fear and excitement coursed from her chest to her limbs. Torin didn't let go, wouldn't let her skitter away, until she melted into him, letting her body grow accustomed to the sensation of being this close to a man.

A man who would be hers.

Her heart leapt at the notion. Surprised at her own body's reaction, she let the idea sink in her mind just as her body sunk into Torin's bare chest. The thrum of his heartbeat resounded deep in his under his muscles, and it appeared to be racing, as though the man himself were just as nervous as she was. The sound was soothing.

'Twas the closest she had ever been to someone other than her mother, or as of late, her brother. Even Lady Elayne was wise enough to keep her distance to accommodate her. Torin, however, enclosed her in his arms, against his chest, to hear his heart, trying to convince her with his massive presence that he was a man she could trust. They held that embrace until the goats in the pen nudged at Caitrin for attention.

***

Torin loosened his embrace but did not let her go. Casting his eyes to her worried face, he struggled to find the right words. Caitrin, surprisingly, had no such troubles.

"What do we do now?" she kept her voice low. 'Twas conspiracy they spoke of. They dared not to have any of Kaleigh's eavesdropping on their private moment.

"I dinna ken," Torin's thick voice confided. He tilted his face up toward the window slits, the pale light dancing across his features. "I've nay prepared a secret wedding 'afore. 'Tis late, that I ken. I dinna think we can get the priest to agree to anything this eve, nor would we have the time. And, I would think ye would rather your mother attended ye?"

His russet eyebrows rose at the question. Caitrin appreciated his consideration of her mother.

"Aye. 'Twould be an injustice to her if I did no' have her at my wedding. Secret though it may be."

"I trust she will keep our secret, aye?"

Caitrin nodded.

"Then we should meet tomorrow. Nay at the kirk. Alighted at night, 'twould assuredly draw the attention of your brother or his men. I will speak with the priest. We shall have our wedding long after nightfall, after most of our kinsmen are well into their drink."

Caitrin nodded as a dreadful thought came over her. Torin's words struck discord.

"Torin, ye are my brother's man. Is this nay a betrayal to him? Wedding his sister against his will? Without his knowledge?"

Seconds passed as Torin looked upon Caitrin, his face hard. True, he knew well 'twould seem a betrayal.

"'Tis nay the first time your brother and I have had a disagreement on how things are done with the clan. Weddings in particular. Just as I had to accept his decisions, including ones that affected me, he will have to do the same. And I come to this decision with the knowledge that I am doing it to save his family. He has just come to know ye. I would no' have him lose ye now."

So, his choice to wed her sprouted from many reasons, much as hers did. Caitrin found solace in knowing it — 'twould seem unfair if he were giving up his freedom, his life, only for her benefit. Nay, he was doing it for himself, and by that same token, for his best friend.

"Come," he said, rising to his feet and lifting her with him. "Ye must tell your mother. And prepare in secret. Ye should have a full wedding, a new dress, flowers, everything that a lass would want on her wedding day, but ye dinna have such luxuries, I'm afraid. Bring only what ye need. I will meet ye behind the barn after most of the men have drunk their fill, when the moon is high, and we will be off to wed."

She nodded and stepped away, but he pulled her back to his chest. Her hand lay upon the dense thatch of hair covering the solid mass of muscle. Her eyes widened into golden saucers as she looked up at him, tense and confused.

"Dinna think," he breathed a bit raggedly, "that I only do this out of honor. Ye are a lass more than fair."

He then dropped his face to hers, pressing his lips against her delicate, pliable mouth in a move so light, so delicate, 'twas as though he wasn't touching her at all. The hairs from his beard tickled at her face, and she softened under his kiss. He pressed his lips against hers once more, a touch more firmly, then loosened his hold again. Torin didn't release her hand but held it as he escorted her from the barn.

"I will see ye tomorrow eve," he promised.

She twirled away, returning to the keep in her bare feet, her shift fluttering behind her, this time resembling less a ghost and more a wedding veil.

***

The hour was late when she finally returned to her own room, the dusky candles she left lit burned down to waxy stubs. Embers from the fire still glowed at the small hearth, providing warmth after Caitrin's escapades out in the chilly night of early spring, dressed in naught but a shift.

Her dirty feet left tracks on the rug by her bed. Sighing at the reminder of how her feet got muddy, she stepped lightly over to her bowl and water pitcher, this time to wash her feet.

On a whim, she pulled back the tapestry that blocked the cold from the window, both hopeful and nervous to see if Torin was again admiring her from below. Her nipples tightened and peaked at the rush of cold, and she didn't care who might see her as she peered into evening.

She didn't think he would be there – 'twas late and they had much to do. In the darkness of deep night, shadows played against the deserted yard, but when she squinted toward the edge of the barn, she could see the giant standing there, his face barely discernible. But he was there, his immense chest bright against the shadows, his face upturned at her window, watching to see that she returned safely to her chambers.

Her breath caught in her chest — the way he watched her at the window, steady and unmoving made her heart flutter. Without thinking, she lifted her hand in a brief wave, and to her surprise, he lifted a large palm in response. Torin remained rooted in his spot until she dropped the tapestry back into place, subtle warmth overtaking the room once more.

What had she done? She questioned herself as she poured a splatter of water into the bowl and whetted the cloth to wash. *Had she truly sworn herself to a man? One she hardly knew? Agreed to a secret marriage against her brother's, her King's, wishes?*

Shaking her head at the audacity of her predicament, she tried to focus on her task. Every time her thoughts moved to her barn encounter with Torin, and what they had agreed to, her spine weakened, and her heart raced. Just the day before she had considered returning to the convent, and now she was betrothed, if secretly. Her own mother did not yet know!

Caitrin flicked her troubled eyes to the door as her mother crossed her thoughts. She should tell her mother straight-away, but 'twas near the middle of night. And as Caitrin finished her ministrations on her feet, she realized just how bone-weary she was. She turned to her bed, slipped her clean toes under the furs, and let sleep slowly overtake her.

'Twas better if she waited on the morn to inform her mother of anything. Caitrin had to consider that Torin may change his mind in the sober light of day. A secret meeting in a barn late at night, who knew what a man might say to a lass? And while he hadn't smelled of whiskey or wine, perchance the man was drunk in his agreement, and he may come to his senses with the morn.

If he were true to his intentions, she would know in the morning. And the fewer people who were aware of their secret plan, the better. How miserable 'twould it be if her brother or the King learned of their treasonous plot before it even happened?

Sleep eluded her as she turned these questions over and over, and 'twas early morning before she finally succumbed to her dreams.

***

Torin also tossed and turned in his bedding that night, but for a starkly different reason. The prospect of such a bonnie lass in his bed kept his cock rigid for much of the evening, and he forced himself to think of sheep to calm his eagerness and find his own sleep. His skin quivered in anticipation of his sudden wedding day, and he hadn't experienced such excitement since before Janet had died. Torin felt like he had lived as only half a man for too long, and now his life was once again full of hope.

And as much as he hated to admit it, that sense of loss was probably the culprit for his boorish behavior when his laird had wed. He hadn't given poor Lady Elayne much of a chance, and while he thought 'twas his general dislike for the loud-mouth lady, he now knew otherwise. 'Twas loneliness tinged with jealousy.

But this night, that chasm of emptiness was filled, replaced with hopes and dreams centered around a buxom blonde lass who seemed to be the object of attention for many.

That Torin, a lowly tacksman, ostler, and disgruntled giant, would win her hand if not yet her heart by stumbling upon her in the barn, shocked him to his core. She was a treasure of the Highlands, and here he was, ready to claim that treasure.

He could not stop the grin that pulled at his lips in his darkened cottage. He would be the envy of every man in the land, a position he had not considered before this eve. That he would claim such a jewel struck him as funny, and he fell asleep with a smile on his face.

Chapter Seven: A Not-So-Secret Wedding

TORIN WOKE WITH the pale sun, practically leaping from his bedding. He barely recognized himself, flushed as he was with the memory of his promise to Caitrin made the night before.

He quickly realized that they had spoken rashly in the barn. Wanting to ensure that Caitrin still desired to wed, that the previous evening wasn't just a drink-induced dream, Torin slipped a tunic over his braies and ran his hands through his curly mass of dark hair in a pathetic attempt to tame the locks. His eyes swiveled around the bailey as he minced across the yard, as quietly as he could for a giant, to the rear door of the kitchens.

Nudging the door ajar, he peeked inside to see if Caitrin were helping prepare the morning meal. Fortune smiled upon him like a thin ray of sunlight — the lass was pounding on oat flour dough as though it had offended her. Catching the smile that again pulled at his bearded lips, Torin cleared his throat, hoping to attract her attention, and hers alone.

'Twas Kaleigh who tossed the door open. Torin cringed. *Did the lassie ken of their plans?* She was quite the eavesdropper, after all. From the look on her face, Torin guessed no; Caitrin had not shared with her what transpired in the barn.

"Torin, what brings ye to the kitchens? No' grabbing a bannock for a meal with the horses?"

Mockery tinged her voice, and he prayed Caitrin didn't hear the insult. He shifted his deep brown gaze past Kaleigh just as Caitrin raised her delicate face to see who visited so early at the door. Her gazed widened at the sight of the mammoth man hunched in the doorway.

"I will speak with him, Kaleigh," Caitrin called out softly as she wiped her hands on a dusty cloth. "Place the bannocks atop the fire, aye?"

While Torin may want to discuss their plot, breaking the morning fast wouldn't wait. Kaleigh, much to her credit, shrugged and nodded, stepping away from the door. Caitrin joined Torin in the garden outside and tugged at the heavy wooden door to ensure 'twas closed. They didn't need Kaleigh's overeager ears listening in.

"Are ye here to change your mind?" Caitrin's voice scarcely rose above a whisper and caught on the light spring breeze which carried it away. Torin, she noted as her eyes roved over the warrior in the full light of morning, did not appear the marrying type. Her own brother had ever joked about his bachelor status in the clan.

Torin shook his head, trying to appear more earnest than frightening. 'Twas obvious the lass feared their plan naught more than a fevered dream, just as he feared when he woke. He wanted to lean closer to her, let his dull heat warm the goose-pimpled flesh below her rolled-up sleeves of her gown. The shaking in his chest calmed when she didn't move away.

"I came to see if ye had reconsidered. Ye were nay in the most rational state yestereve," he said.

Caitrin flicked a cautious gaze at Torin. She couldn't tell if he was patronizing her, but his earnest, handsome face didn't appear to find jest at her predicament. Or in their secret plot. She nodded instead, airy tendrils of honey-colored hair waving in the breeze. Torin needed to resist the urge to tuck one bright lock behind her ear.

Their hushed conversation made the peace of the garden more prominent. After so many months with the brash MacCollough clan, Caitrin had learned that silence can speak louder than words. She liked that Torin also appreciated quiet. Torin took advantage of the tranquil moment and reached for Caitrin's hand, hoping that, in the stark light of day, she wouldn't shy away.

He was rewarded. Her dainty hand was lost in his palm as she let it rest in his warm grasp. Though she kept her eyes averted, their touching hands spoke volumes.

"If ye are still agreed, Cait, then so am I. 'Twould be my honor to wed ye, to help ye avoid a forced wedding to a strange man." His words eased her nervous heart.

Caitrin inhaled a deep, cleansing breath. "Aye, I am still agreed."

Torin gave a curt nod and her hand a gentle squeeze. "Then tonight, we should meet here, in the garden, long after supper. Once the men are well into their cups and the moon is high." He turned his face skyward, noting the clouds above. "Should we be able to see the moon, that is. I will wait on ye."

She turned her head slightly, and he admired her graceful profile — her pert nose, her full lips. "And ye shall speak with the Priest? Will he agree?" she asked.

"Aye," Torin nodded again. "He's a good man who would no sooner want to see a lass wed against her will than the devil walk this land. He's a bit of a confidant of mine and does no' turn down good coin. I will speak with him directly."

"May I bring my mam?" Her question was almost childlike, and Torin's heart constricted painfully at the fear she must feel in being a pawn subjected to the whims of men. He would deny her nothing.

"Aye, lassie. We shall need witnesses, ye ken?"

Relief flooded her features, smoothing the worry lines that had pulled at her forehead. She looked, well, happy.

"I will tell my mam later today. Better to keep as much of this to ourselves for as long as possible, aye?" She raised a tawny eyebrow at him, a move that so resembled her brother Torin was taken aback.

Her gesture reminded him that he was going behind his Laird's back, a type of betrayal of his closest friend, in wedding Caitrin. Torin steeled his resolve, telling himself that he was saving the lass, and thus working on behalf of his laird's best interest. 'Twasn't a full lie, but the shaded half-truth needed to be enough to keep him on this track. Well, that, and the stunning golden loveliness of the woman standing by his side.

A rustling sound burst from the kitchens, and they turned to see Kaleigh peeking from around the doorway, her bright blue eyes wide. Torin caught Caitrin's gaze, dropped her hand, and marched off toward the stables without a look back.

Caitrin reentered the kitchens, laying her hand on Kaleigh's arm. "Dinna say a word, please."

Kaleigh's face worked to suppress a smile. "Will ye tell me later?" she pried.

Caitrin sighed, her own heart warming at the friendly banter from the woman who mayhap saved her from a dire future. A young woman she may very well consider her first friend. "Aye, Kay. That I will."

Kaleigh wrapped her arm around Caitrin's waist as they returned to the steamy work of the kitchens.

***

Caitrin was on edge the whole day, biting at her nubby nails out of nervous habit. Going behind her brother's back and against the will of the King, and wedding a man she barely knew, was enough to unnerve anyone.

'Twas close to the evening meal before Caitrin was able to search out her mother and share her plan with Torin. Davina was reclining in her room, resting from her day of work. She scarcely heard Caitrin's words as the lass stood facing the fire, speaking in her light voice.

Davina shot up straight on her bed. "My daughter, what did ye say?"

Caitrin cringed, turning from the hearth to repeat herself.

"Torin has agreed to wed me to save me from the King's plot to barter me off. He is a good man, one I at least ken. We shall meet with the priest this eve and wed. Torin agreed that ye, as the mother of an only daughter, should be there, but it must remain a secret. Will ye join me? We will meet Torin outside the kitchens tonight once the King and most of his men are well in their drink."

Davina clutched at her chest, her mouth gaping like a landed fish. Her skittish, nervous lass, the one who considered taking a nun's vows, was running off to wed the local tacksman? She would have sat down hard if she had not already been seated.

"Tonight?" Davina managed squeak out.

Caitrin nodded, picking at her woolen skirts. Silence hung between them as Caitrin waited for her mother's response, and as Davina tried to find some sense in what her daughter just told her.

"Tonight," she repeated. Caitrin tipped her delicate features toward her mother, her eyes averted. Her plan was solid, yet she feared her mother's reaction.

"Tonight?" she asked once more.

"Mother—" Caitrin pleaded. Davina waved her off.

"Aye, my daughter. Ye must ken my surprise. Did ye plan to wed the lad afore this?"

Caitrin pursed her lips, and Davina had her answer. But having her daughter wed a local man would keep her daughter close, and Torin was her son's dearest friend and adviser. It could be worse, Davina knew. So much worse. She sighed and her face softened at Caitrin.

"Weel, we canna have ye wed in your work shift! *Wheest*! What shall we find ye to wear for your wedding day?"

Excitement rose within Davina's chest, replacing the shock. As much as this was a rushed wedding, 'twas her daughter's wedding, nonetheless. She wanted it to be as proper as possible.

"Come lassie," Davina grabbed Caitrin by her upper arm and all but dragged Caitrin to her own chamber where she dug through Caitrin's trunk.

"We must find ye a decent gown. And after the evening meal, we will coif your hair so 'tis a golden halo, the likes of which the Torin lad has never seen. He will be smitten. What can we use for a ring?"

Caitrin stood forlorn in the middle of her chambers, watching her mother tear through her room in a storm. A light knock at the chamber door caused them both to still their movements. They shared an anxious look before Caitrin stepped to the door.

Kaleigh burst into the room, a broad smile plastered across her face.

"I've seen ye, Caitrin," Kaleigh gushed. "Torin has a solution for ye, aye? He is to wed ye?"

Every last bit of color drained from Caitrin's face. *How had she learned of their plan?* She began to shake, fearing her and Torin's plan was discovered. Kaleigh patted Caitrin on the shoulder and giggled.

"Ooch, dinna fash, Cait," Kaleigh comforted her. "Your secret's safe with me. I guessed after I saw ye with Torin in the gardens."

She flicked her sparkling blue gaze from Caitrin to Davina. "Are ye looking for a proper gown for her? If ye like, I can get ye the one I wore last year. It should fit ye well, mayhap a bit short."

Kaleigh bounced on her toes, ready to rush off for the dress. Davina barely finished nodding before Kaleigh ran out the door toward her own croft she shared with Duncan.

"Weel, we have a gown. The noise below tells me the evening meal should be served soon. Let us complete our work so we can retire here as soon as the meal is over and get ye ready."

Davina stepped to her daughter, hugging her in a tight embrace. Caitrin returned the gesture, clinging to her mother. Even though the plan was underway, their secret still sent shivers of fear through her veins, and she found solace in her mother's arms.

"Tis no' what I hoped for your wedding day," Davina whispered in Caitrin's ear, "but we shall make a fine wedding for ye."

***

That night, after the carousing of the clansmen steadied to an unobtrusive din, Davina and Caitrin escaped to the peace and quiet of Caitrin's room to resume their perfidy. Caitrin scrubbed the remnants of the kitchen work off her skin while her mother again rooted through Caitrin's trunk for her cleanest shift. She also unearthed several ribbons from Caitrin's girlhood, and a fresh MacCollough plaid that would do well for a wedding.

They weren't surprised at the knock at the door, but their eyes widened as Lady Elayne entered like a stately queen, followed by a sheepish Kaleigh holding a simple blue gown. The young woman closed the door as Elayne surveyed the women in the room. Her stoic stare was unreadable, and everyone was frozen as they waited for the shrieking ire of the Lady of the keep. They were caught — the Lady would surely report them to Declan, and they had no defense for their actions.

Just as Davina lifted her head to speak, Elayne's sharp, silvery eyes softened. She stepped to Caitrin, catching the frightened lassie in her arms.

"Oh Caitrin, dinna fash. I forced Kaleigh to share her secret. I noticed ye seemed distracted all day. I saw her carrying her gown, and Kaleigh could nay keep a secret if her life depended on it."

"Ooch!" Kaleigh squealed in protest. Elayne cut her eyes to the dainty lass.

"Dinna act affronted, Kaleigh. Ye ken every emotion shows on your face. Ye have no guile to speak of." Elayne turned her attention to Caitrin, gazing down on her sister-by-law.

"Torin, eh?" Elayne shook her head, managing to hide the surprise on her face.

Of all the men in the clan, Torin was the last she expected to rise to the occasion of marriage. After the death of his bairn and his hand-fast wife, he was hesitant to give his heart to anyone, save the Laird Declan MacCollough himself. But here was this timid, unassuming lass, and she managed to break down the stone wall Torin had built so solidly around his heart.

Elayne regarded the blue gown draped over Kaleigh's arm. She exhaled heavily, knowing she would well regret her next action.

"The blue gown? Nay, 'twill no' do for the Laird's sister. Kaleigh, my husband is still below. Can ye go to my chambers and retrieve my yellow gown? The one edged in gold trim?"

Kaleigh dropped the blue dress on the trunk as she ran from the room at her Lady's command, once again flitting like an excited little bird.

"And my dress will be long enough, for certain," Elayne shrugged as she spoke. Though Caitrin was slender and tall for a woman, she was nothing compared to Elayne's height. And for a wedding, a longer gown would be more appropriate. "And the yellow and gold will flatter ye well."

Davina and Caitrin continued to stare in shocked silence. Their fears that Lady Elayne would retrieve Declan and their deceptions would be discovered were for naught. Instead, here the lady stood, commanding Caitrin's upcoming secret nuptials.

"Ye are no' going to say anything to Declan?" Davina asked.

Elayne shrugged again. "I will have to tell my husband soon, ye ken. But for tonight, I will help ye wed the giant. I ken King Robert will avail himself of any opportunity to form alliances, and right now, Caitrin is one of those opportunities. It happens far too often. I canna permit a woman to become a bartering chip — no' if I can help it. I was able to choose my husband, and I would want the same for ye, sister-by-law."

Caitrin visibly shook as her fretting abated. If Lady Elayne sanctioned her wedding, perchance she could head off

Declan's anger, assuage any claims of betrayal. Let Lady Elayne deal with the Laird.

"Weel, we have to get ye ready, daughter," Davina clapped her hands. "I will brush out your hair, and ye can wear this shift."

Elayne leaned near the door to stand guard and await Kaleigh. The young woman barged through the door just as Caitrin pulled the creamy shift over her head.

The women helped Caitrin into the dress. 'Twas a bit long, as Elayne predicted, but once they cinched the gold cord along her ribs in the front, the dress fit flawlessly. The soft yellow fabric fell in a gentle line over her hips and dragged on the rushes of the floor. Up thrust by the cinched waist, her plump breasts filled the gathered shift, the pale swells playing peek-a-boo as she breathed.

Once the gown was in place, Kaleigh and Davina wrapped her thick golden hair into a coronet around her head, weaving a rainbow of ribbons through her locks. Then they draped the fresh green and black tartan over her shoulder, where the dun colors made the yellow and gold appear brighter. The effect was stunning, and when she stood, she could have been mistaken for a Lady herself. Both Kaleigh and Lady Elayne told her as much as they ushered her out to the hall.

Playing lookout as they descended the stair, Kaleigh and Elayne exited the kitchen door, Caitrin right behind with Davina pushing against her back as encouragement. She stumbled into the garden, and a shadow of surprise passed over Torin's face, hardly visible under his dark beard this late in the night.

"What's all this?" Torin's voice could not hide his shock. "We have an audience for something that should have been a secret?" His dark gaze caught Elayne's, challenging her to run to Declan and snitch on them.

Elayne waved her hand at Torin. "Dinna fret, ye large beast of a man," she teased. "I am no' here to report ye to my husband. I'm here to help ye succeed. Now, where is this priest ye claim to have?"

"Aye, where is this priest?" a voice from the side of the garden called out. They all turned in surprise, and Kaleigh gasped as she saw her husband, Duncan, step from the shadows.

"Ooch, Duncan," Elayne greeted the man unperturbed. "So ye, too, have found us out."

Duncan shifted his eyes to Kaleigh who stood at Elayne's side, and then back to the giant man who appeared cleaner than Duncan had seen in nigh a fortnight.

"'Twould seem so," Duncan drawled. "Kaleigh, do ye wish to tell your husband the reason for all the sneaking about? Ye did no' hide it well."

Elayne lifted her eyes to the evening sky in agreement.

"Husband," Kaleigh began in a little voice. "I can explain . . ."

"She was helping me," Elayne interrupted, attempting to save the lass from any conflict with her husband. She shielded the young woman with her arm. "We are having a wedding tonight, between Torin and the lass here, and we would rather Declan no' ken until the deed is done."

Elayne's voice was stern, offering no chance to disagree. Duncan's eyebrows reached his hairline. He stepped to Torin and clapped him on the back. To his credit, the giant stumbled under the force of the pounding.

"Torin, ye cad! I had no' thought it in ye! Why did ye no' tell me? As your oldest friend, I would no' forgo such a grand event! Ye need a man to stand with ye, Torin. And 'tis tonight? Weel, let's get ye to the priest then."

Torin cringed at his kinsman's booming voice that carried across the gardens but was inwardly pleased that one of his kinsmen wanted to stand by his side. He would need that support when Declan tried to pummel him in the barn tomorrow. Swiveling his head around, he worried they had attracted attention. They had tarried too long in the gardens as 'twas, in Torin's estimation. And now with a crowd of escorts? They would attract more attention, without a doubt. A nuance of fear sprung in his chest.

"Come, ye all! Quit your dawdling. We have a wedding to attend!" Elayne flapped her hands at those gathered, waving them toward the recesses of the gardens and the trees beyond. When she stepped forward, Torin could see behind her, and his breath caught at the golden vision of Caitrin.

Even in the dark of night, she seemed to glow, like a fire burned from within her, and that fire lit a fuse within Torin. Everything in the garden, including the spring moon above, dimmed in Caitrin's radiance. She stood as regal as a goddess, her head held unusually high. Her hair, wrapped in heavy ropes around her head, ended in gentle curls that fell down her neck and back. Torin was thunderstruck, rooted to his spot, unable to tear his gaze away.

Until Duncan smacked the back of his head and pulled on his tunic, yanking him toward the far side of the gardens.

***

Torin led the small entourage deep into the woods beyond the stables. Once the firelight from *BlackBraes* was no longer in sight, Torin lit a small torch to help the pale moonlight guide their way.

As they marched, Caitrin flicked her eyes forward to admire Torin with a surreptitious gaze. He seemed to stand even taller, if such a thing were possible. His chestnut-brown tunic appeared freshly washed, his trews clean and gathered tightly in his boots, and the tartan draped over his shoulders matched her own. Even his riotous hair, usually standing on end in a russet chaos of locks, was tamed, brushed into smooth waves that reached past his neck. She imagined that, instead of the smell of horses that he usually carried with him, he would give off a soapy scent.

The trees opened to a small glen where a young man in a white robe waited impatiently. He jumped when they came upon them, ogling the throng.

"Torin! Ye said ye would bring the bride and her mam! What's all this?" The priest's eyes widened when he recognized Lady Elayne. "Milady! Ooch! 'Tis nay what ye think!"

Elayne chuckled and stepped close to the priest. "Ye are wrong. 'Tis exactly what I think. Or at least it'd better be, for all our sakes. I would hate for us to be caught doing nothing in the glen this late on a fine spring evening."

The priest shifted his frightened gaze back and forth between Elayne and Torin, and deciding to keep his promise, he held his hand toward the enormous man.

"Ooch, weel, then. Torin, my lad. Is your bride with ye?"

"Aye, Father." Torin shifted to the side so Caitrin could step forward. The priest's wry grin of approval escaped, and Torin caught it with a twitch of his own mouth.

"Witnesses?" the priest called out. Davina, Elayne, Kaleigh, and Duncan moved to flank the couple, and the rites began.

In the stillness of the night, their vows carried on the cool air, as though their union was part of nature's great plan. The mood was galvanizing, so much so that Caitrin didn't flinch when the priest cut her palm and pressed it to Torin's, mixing their blood, binding them for life.

"Do ye have any rings?"

Caitrin nearly fainted. In the bustling with Elayne and getting dressed, she forgot to ask her mother about a ring. She had naught for her new husband. What way was that to start a marriage?

Before she could answer, Elayne leaned in and set a bronze circlet in her hand. She nodded and patted Caitrin's hand, smiling at the lass. 'Twas little more than a trinket, but the gesture was kind. Blinking back tears, Caitrin let out a sigh of relief and mouthed a silent *thank you* at her sister-by-law. A gentle smile rested on Elayne's lips in response.

The bronze ring she slid on Torin's finger caught on his thick knuckle, and Caitrin feared 'twould not fit. Would that be a bad omen? At the last second, Torin wiggled his finger, and the band forced itself over, fitting snuggly against his skin.

As for Torin, he withdrew a silver ring for Caitrin, one he prayed would fit her slender finger. The one he had planned for his hand-fast wife was buried with her in her shroud, not that he would have used that cursed ring with this second chance. He had purchased this ring from the smithy, who took care to etch a dainty filigree along the outer edge. The cost was dear, but not nearly worth a bride like Caitrin.

With their right hands wrapped in plaid and their left hands banded with rings, the priest told Torin 'twas time to kiss his bride. Everyone's breath, it seemed to Torin, caught in anticipation. With such an innocent, even a kiss could be harrowing. Torin pressed close to Caitrin, waiting for her to shrink away, but Caitrin stood erect before him, awaiting his kiss.

Her eyes never left his face as he crossed that short chasm between them and brushed his lips across hers. Just as their lips met, he slid his arm around her waist, drawing her body taut against his. Her breasts pressed firmly against his chest. His beard tickled her chin, and she was correct; he did smell of a grassy soap. She reached her free arm to his shoulder, clutching him just as he did her.

Too soon the kiss was over, and her mind spun as Torin pulled away, the low cheering of their family echoing in his ears. 'Twas done. They were wed. And when he admired his bride once more, he was amazed at her bright eyes and subtle smile. Caitrin, to his delight, looked pleased about it.

***

Their small collections of witnesses, including the priest, marched back to *BlackBraes*. Elayne caught up with Torin, leaning into his ear to make herself heard.

"Ye surprised me, Torin. Knowing your history and the like."

"Mmmm," Torin grumbled, not wanting to be reminded. He wanted his attentions centered on the blonde vision who held his other arm. "And ye surprised me," he responded. "I would no' ken ye to help me wed outside Declan's knowledge, what with our history *and the like*."

Elayne shrugged off his suggestive comment. "We made our peace. And in the pursuit of your happiness, Torin, I shall always ride to your side. Though ye may no' care for me overmuch, ye are my husband's man, and your happiness, and his sister's, bring him much joy."

"Mmmm," Torin mumbled again.

Lady Elayne was astute in regards to her husband's desires. Declan was not a complicated man, and he wanted his kinsmen to have what he had — a home, a wife, a family, a peaceful existence. What man did not want such simple desires?

She patted him on the back, mimicking Duncan's earlier gesture. "But be warned, Torin, I shall have to break the news to Declan once I return, if the Laird himself does no' meet us at your door. Ye should make this marriage, um, official, quickly. Tonight."

One elegant eyebrow rose in the darkness, and Torin twisted his head away from her less-than-subtle implication to watch Caitrin walking next to him. The lass had to muster all her courage to kiss. How could he bed her?

Elayne left Torin's side, taking the lead near the priest. Their heads inclined as they spoke lowly, with Elayne most likely commanding the good priest to ensure this marriage was as unbreakable as possible. Elayne wouldn't put her reputation on the line if she thought 'twould not end well for her. She wanted this marriage to end well.

Torin struggled with Lady Elayne's parting words. He'd promised himself he would not touch the lass until she came to him, open and wanting. Though 'twould absolutely drive him to the brink of madness, Torin intended to be the most chaste husband until his new bride was comfortable enough with him to welcome him to her bed. He did not want an ice-cold, fearful virgin between the sheets.

But Elayne's command dictated a different course of action. Would Declan, or God help him, the King, discredit their wedding vows if they did not consummate the marriage? Could that force Declan's hand, causing the King to barter her off as rapidly as possible?

With Declan, the choice would be easy, but regarding the King . . . Torin sighed heavily as the flames from the MacCollough stronghold blossomed beyond the dense thicket of trees. King Robert was another matter, and if Torin truly wanted to keep the lass safe at her brother's keep, he had only one option before him.

He would have to make Caitrin comfortable and wanting before the sun rose the following morn.

Chapter Eight: A Husband's Bed

CAITRIN HAD REMAINED wordless during the walk back to *BlackBraes*. Whether she was in shock that she was actually wedded, or in fear that she may have betrayed her brother, or nervous that she must now lie with a man, she couldn't tell. As they made their way through the trees, she stole small glances in Torin's direction, trying to understand the giant and her own roiling emotions. Perchance one day he could open up and admit the full truth of why he wedded her.

At the entrance to the gardens, Davina and Kaleigh hugged Caitrin and went their separate ways — Davina into the recesses of the keep and Kaleigh with Duncan towards their simple cottage. Caitrin's watery hazel gaze followed Davina as she departed. For the first time in her life, Caitrin would not reside in the same home as her mother. She bit the inside of her lip to keep her emotions under control and stop herself from running after her like a lost puppy. Instead she turned her head to Torin, her new husband.

Duncan pounded Torin on the back one last time and gave him a suggestive wink before placing his arm around Kaleigh's waist. The priest had readily gone his separate way before they exited the trees, to his own tiny home near the village church, trying to put as much distance between this treasonous night and himself as he could.

Torin was still amazed the priest had agreed to perform the marriage at all. Father MacNally may be loyal to his Laird and his King, but he was a devout priest, and from his perspective, the games of men did not supersede the will of God. He put a marriage sacrament above the will of the King any day, and for that, Torin was grateful.

'Twas late when they reached Torin's cottage adjacent to the rear of the stables. Though she'd spent her entire life by her mother's side, curiosity overshadowed Caitrin's fear and nerves. She was prepared to see her new home for the first time, and she held no compunctions about the state the home would be in. She'd be fortunate if they were not sleeping on a dirt floor.

Surprise flashed across Caitrin's face when she stepped through the sturdy wood and iron door. Instead of a mangy, dirt encrusted home, typical of most crofts she had come across, she found the cottage to be neat, every pot and bowl in its place, a woolen coverlet pulled over the bedding along the far side of the croft, separated from the main living area by a hanging sheet.

The hearth to the side of the tidy table showed peat stain from use but was otherwise as tidy as the rest of the cottage. Two large woven mats, one on the floor of the living area and a smaller one along the edge of the bedding, made the cold, stone croft feel homey.

Much to Caitrin's delight, she noted a freshly hewn table of young ash wood set at the foot of the bedding curtain, topped with a clean bowl and a wooden pitcher of clear water – a table similar to the very one she left behind at the keep. A short stack of linen cloths perched on the edge of the table, obviously new and, she assumed, a welcoming gift for her. *How long had he worked on it?* she wondered. Caitrin's mouth curved into an unconscious smile at the effort Torin put forth to make the house fit for her.

His bedding, tucked against the wall adjacent to the stables, drew Caitrin's attention again. Her joyous smile faltered, knowing full well that she would soon lie with this giant of a man on that bed. Her eyes kept flitting back to it with tense expectation.

Torin had bolted the door against the wilds of the outdoors, with only the snapping and crackling of the low fire breaking the tranquil room. Stepping lightly for a man of his size, Torin ducked under a support beam to the fire, feeding it with dry kindling and peat. The fire blazed for a fierce moment, its warmth chasing away the chill of their evening adventures.

***

Torin gestured for Caitrin to sit on the bed, and she balanced on the edge, arranging her gold dress as she sat. Torin's weight bowed the bedding as he joined her, close but not quite touching. Caitrin hazarded a guess that Torin seemed as nervous as she. In a deft move, he grabbed her hand, cradling it on his lap. His grizzled face softened as he spoke.

"I wish we had more time," he said into the peat-infused air of the cottage. Caitrin's other hand rested on her bosom, not understanding. She leaned into him.

"Time for what? I ken what tonight means, but how long —?"

She couldn't ask the question aloud, as blushing and embarrassment overcame her. Blushing to the roots of her hair, Caitrin, and her pink cheeks that made her skin glow, pulled at Torin's heart. He patted her hand, a shy smile peeking from under his thick beard.

"Nay lassie, 'tis no' what I mean." He inhaled deeply, his gigantic chest inflating to an even larger girth. *He was nervous!* Caitrin realized, her eyes widening. "I wish I'd the time to woo ye."

"But we are wed. Why do ye need time for that? How much time do we need?"

Torin titled his head to catch her wide, golden gaze that screamed innocence. She was a vision of perfection in her borrowed yellow gown. Her beauty was stunning, especially in the low light of the fire, and she had nary a notion of her effect on him. *Oh, Lord in Heaven.* He was in for a trial this night.

"Wooing is more than just anticipation of marriage," Torin continued. "Wooing is, uh, to encourage excitement. To build passion. A passion that rises until it's consummated on a wedding night, or any night a man and wife spend in bed. Ye deserve that, to be stroked, to feel that building passion. I fear this night will no' be the most welcome, I will no' be welcome, because ye didn't get to feel that passion build over time."

"'Twas it like that for ye and your wife? Janet?"

It seemed strange to talk of his handfast wife with his new wife on their wedding night. Torin's insides cringed and folded in sharp agony at the sound of his handfast wife's name. They were young when they met and fell in love, and their love for each other was inflamed by those passions of youth. When she died, he'd had the misguided sense of nobility to think he wouldn't lie with another woman again.

That lasted about a month before he sought solace with a local whore. 'Twasn't the same, he felt that well, and only bedded a willing woman when his need built to a screaming crescendo. But to woo another? Wed another? To share a loving embrace? Share that intimacy? As he grew older, he understood the folly of his youthful vow to never love again. Yet, here he was, having vowed before God to love and protect this woman, and she deserved to be loved, as wholly and passionately as a woman should be. At least on his end, Torin had a good start on loving passion, but he wanted Caitrin to feel the same.

"Aye," he finally answered. "We wooed and loved much. But with ye, I would give ye the same, more, now."

He turned on the bedding to admire her delicate features as he made another vow to her — one that he would take more to heart than even the vow they just made before the priest. "I am older, I ken more of the world, of women, but no' perchance about love. I would have us travel that road together. Ye deserve that. I would have us be passionate and loving with each other."

His heartfelt words were heavy with emotion and tore at Caitrin, her heart weeping for the man who suffered such a loss, lived as half a man, and presently forced his own hand to wed again to save her from an uncertain fate. Just as he said she deserved to be wooed and loved, so did this giant man before her, even if he didn't know it.

Caitrin studied his face, making her own silent vow to be as good a wife, in all ways possible, to the gentle giant who was now her husband. Torin sacrificed much for her, and she vowed to do the same. Placing her other hand over his, she entwined their fingers. 'Twas the boldest move she'd taken with a man, with any person. And she felt the heat of his racing blood flow through his hands and arms. Yet, he still didn't move any closer.

He was letting her take the lead. Caitrin could see 'twas taking every effort to stay rooted in his spot, out of respect for her. His giant body was naught more than a shell to the world that instead contained a soft, caring man.

"Then why don't ye woo me now?" she asked in a hushed tone.

Torin's dark eyes narrowed. "What, now? We are already at the bed, and we must finish this tonight. We dinna have time —?"

"Is there a time limit for wooing?" she asked, her fair brow crinkling with curiosity. What she knew of wooing wouldn't fill a broken eggshell. "Can we just woo, but more quickly? What would ye have done if ye wanted to woo me, starting when we met in the barn?"

Now his eye widened, a tender look of understanding crossing his features. He lifted her hand to his lips.

"First, I would have taken your hand," he explained behind her fingertips, "perchance to help ye rise from a stool. I would have tried to sniff your hair as ye rose, catching hints of heather and grass, bright scents in the dank air, and I would have kissed your hand once ye had your feet."

Then he did just that, starting at her fingertips and working his way to her palm with his furry lips that tickled her skin. Caitrin shivered at the delicate sensation of his lips. Her chest heaved, pressing her breasts up against the kirtle that threatened to burst. Her cleavage deepened, and her head spun at the intimacy of something as simple as a kiss on the hand.

"What would ye do next?" Her voice was little more than a husky whisper.

"I would hope ye would stand close to me, perchance the next time I caught ye in the barn," Torin continued in his patient, rough voice. "If ye did, I would lean in, trying to touch as much of ye as I could without frightening ye. And if ye didn't skitter away, I would bring my head down to kiss you in that milky curve of your neck."

He didn't move. He waited to see if she would squirm away from his forward words. Caitrin remained where she was, instead tipping her head imperceptibly to one side. Her golden waves in the intricately braided coiffure exposed much of her neck already, and now she was offering him more.

Torin was unable to stop the groan that pulled from his ballocks up through his chest. He shifted, moving as near to her as he could while still seated and facing her. Brushing his fingers over her neck to sweep away a shiny, rogue lock of hair, he then marked that same place with his mouth, using his tongue to lick gently before sucking on her milky skin. From her, he drew a quivering moan, one she attempted to hide, but it still managed to escape.

Lifting his lips from her skin, his beard prickled, and she shivered once more. Every part of her skin reacted, puckering, and Torin let his eyes drop to her breasts to enjoy the small outline of her nipples against the dainty fabric of the dress. His restraint, he thought to himself, was remarkable — all he wanted to do was rip that fabric from her body.

Keeping his actions at bay caused his own shaking as he pulled back. She kept her eyes hooded and didn't speak, and Torin feared he went too far. But he'd have to go farther before the night was over.

"Cait?" He kept his voice as low as possible, fearing a skittish reaction. That she was still on the bed with him was shocking enough. Would she encourage him?

"Yes," she answered with a shaky voice. "Ye would have wooed me well, methinks." She took a sharp breath in through her nose, strengthening her resolve. She was fearful, aye, but the touch of his lips on her skin was exciting, and she liked it. "And what would ye have done next, Torin, to woo me?"

His name on her enticing pink lips nearly sent him over the edge. Torin gripped the bedding as he answered.

"I would try to take it too far," he admitted, breathless. "And I'd hope ye would let me."

She said nothing, but shifted closer to him, waiting for him to show her how far he would try. She closed her eyes, and the mounds of her breasts heaved with her nervous, fervent breathing.

Reminding himself over and over to go slow, slower than he thought humanly possible, Torin ran his large fingers across the lacy edge of her kirtle that struggled to contain her breasts. Caitrin did react, shying away with shock, then returning to her position so his fingers could continue to grace her skin. Her whole body vibrated like a witching rod, as though it called out for Torin.

He brushed his fingers over that lace edging several times, then slowly worked a finger under the ribbon that held the neckline closed. With his other hand, he pulled at the yellow ribbon, exposing most of her breasts to his view. Only the nipples caught, still hidden under the creamy fabric.

"Here ye would stop me," he told her as he placed his hand over the fullness of her breast. The nipple pulled even more taut against his palm. "Ye would take my hand and pull it away with a sly smile that promised more later."

Even with every nerve on fire, she forced herself to be still and pliant under his hands. Caitrin peeked at him with one eye and felt a leisurely smile flow across her face. She had never been so excited and frightened at the same time. Her body wanted to both run away and press closer, and the confusion only made her head swim all the more. But she didn't pull away.

"But if ye didn't run away," he continued with that same breathless voice, "I would risk a full kiss, and try to press my advantage as much as ye would allow."

Again, she surprised him by lifting her head just a bit, presenting her full pink lips, and Torin felt any self-control he had left waver. With one giant hand on her full breast, he wrapped the other around her waist and crushed her into him, his mouth finding hers in a frenzy of kissing, his tongue licking past her lips to play against her tongue. He wanted to know her, taste and feel every part of her, and this slow wooing dance was killing him.

The warmth of his muscular arms was so male, so bracing. She didn't put her arms around him, nor did she beat on his chest to force him away. Her hand rested lightly on his shoulder, as if waiting, testing the waters.

Torin forced himself away for fear he would push her onto the bed, hike up her skirts, and take her without a thought. His cock was demanding, trying to take over his more rational mind, and he had to fight hard to regain control.

"Cait, I'm sorry," he started. Caitrin pressed a fingertip to his lip.

"Nay, dinna be sorry. If ye are honest with me, is this how ye would woo me? If aye, then woo me. Dinna stop now, please."

'Twas the *please* that did him in. She knew what needed to be done, and she wanted to be as ready for it as possible. Only Torin could do that for her.

"What would ye do next, if ye were wooing me? If I let ye go a tad farther than we should have?" Her voice may have wavered, but her commitment to him was jolting.

Pride and desired filled him at her encouragement. She was timid beyond understanding, and this night was probably one of the most frightening she would ever endure, and she had to have it with him. Yet here she was encouraging him, helping him to keep his vow to love her as she should be loved. Her beauty, the stunning nature of her ran more than skin deep. Torin was a fortunate man, to be sure. He tilted his head to hers.

***

Torin's lips slipped from her mouth to her neck, his practiced tongue sweeping and dipping at every perfect spot. Caitrin shivered and felt her defenses weaken. How did he know exactly where to lick? Where to touch? How did he have such an effect on her, when she didn't know such actions even existed?

Distracted by the attentions of his tongue, she didn't notice he pulled the kirtle and her gown below her taut breasts, his fingertips brushing at her curves with feathery touches.

"I would convince ye to do more, using my lips and tongue," his deep baritone whispered into her ear, sending another flurry of shivers across her spine. "I would lick and touch ye everywhere, until your mind was nay longer yours and ye permitted me access to all of ye."

His fingers now worked at the silken gold cord that held her gown together – that slender piece of fabric was all that kept her naked skin from Torin's advances. As his lips and tongue continued their assault on Caitrin's lips and neck, Torin cautiously slid the sleeves of the gown down her arms. Using minute movements so as not to frighten her, Torin managed to work her gown to her waist, exposing her perfectly rounded breasts to his view.

It took a moment for her brain to realize she was uncovered in front of him, and her arms crossed over her chest in a chaste gesture. Instead of pulling her arms away, Torin sat up straight on the bed.

"Then, I would offer myself to ye. I cannot woo ye unless ye want me to. Now 'twould be my turn to expose myself, all of me, to ye."

His burnished tunic and rich plaid flew off his shoulders with one easy flick of his arms. He slipped his leather shoes off his feet, and turned, his broad shoulders and chest just as bare as hers.

Well, not quite as bare. A swirled mat of dark hair covered the wide expanse of his chest and matched the hair of his head and beard. Caitrin stared at that muscled chest, in awe at how close she was to a near-naked man. Her golden eyes flicked from his chest to his encouraging eyes and back to that chest. Just looking at him before her made her heart flutter.

She lifted a tentative hand from her own nakedness, her fingers reaching out to touch him. Only a scant centimeter from his chest she paused, flicking her questioning eyes back to his face. Torin nodded.

"I am yours, Caitrin," he whispered haggardly, the patience of their intimacy trying him to the very brink of madness. If only she knew just how much power she held over him. He would do anything to have her fingers touch his skin.

And then they did. Her dainty fingertips ran through is chest hair, pressing against the solid wall of muscle hidden beneath. Torin's own breath caught, and Caitrin noticed, a pull of a smile softening the apprehensive look on her face.

"Ye react like I do," she commented. Torin held his breath as her fingertips continued their assault on his skin, flicking across his nipples. He thought he would burst out of his trews.

"Then I would finish undressing, both ye and myself."

Caitrin yanked her hand back as though she touched fire. And that wasn't an impossible idea. She did indeed play with fire when she touched him — she just didn't know it.

Torin rose slightly from the bedding, slipping his trews off his legs in one fluid move. Caitrin's eyes couldn't stop staring at his rounded buttocks, as chiseled as firm stone, or the burgeoning flesh that protruded below his waist. He sat back on the bed.

Instead of pressing his need, pushing her into the bed and claiming her as his wife, he resumed his soft assault on her lips, licking and kissing again until her arms, and her defenses, dropped.

"I am exposed for ye, at your mercy, wife," he breathed into her ear, drawing a finger down her neck to the tops of her breasts. Her nervous, excited shivers resumed.

Caitrin's own hands moved almost without her guidance, resting on the mass of muscular thigh that pressed against her skirts. The sensation of his finger, so light and gentle for such a giant of a man, made her throw her head back, exposing her breasts to him fully. Only then did Torin shift his head, capturing a pink nipple in his lips. She gasped with surprise and grabbed at his head, the heat of his lips unlike any sensation she'd ever experienced. Despite her better judgment, she found herself wriggling, writhing under his ministration, wanting more of something she couldn't comprehend.

Torin slipped his hand under her waist, working the gown off her hips and legs, letting it slip to the ground. Caitrin panted, and though she noticed her complete lack of clothing, her mind buzzed and spun from Torin's attentions, and she didn't care. *He's my husband,* her mind flashed, and when his hand moved between her legs, she didn't try to skitter away. In fact, her legs wanted to open, wanted his hand there. Her own brash behavior surprised her, but was lost in the swirl of sensations, feelings, and headiness Torin worked upon her.

"Now I would take my reward," he said into her lips as he caressed them with his own.

His beard was both rough and exciting, rubbing against her skin, marking her as his own. Then his thick legs were between her milky white thighs, and she felt a probing at her opening. He was gigantic — his body, his chest, his legs, his member — and a moue of panic moved through her. How could she be with a man who was a giant among men? Her breath caught, and Torin noticed her sudden burst of fear.

He didn't stop his kisses or caresses, but worked them more, whispering into her ear terms of love and endearments.

"I will be gentle with ye, wife. 'Twill be a moment of pain, but I will do all I can to remedy that."

Then he shifted and entered her in a swift movement. She was ready, which helped significantly, but she was also tight, so tight, and she cried out at the breach.

"'Tis the worst, lass," he whispered, nuzzling his face into the sweaty curve of her neck.

He worked at calming her, making her excited for him again after the shocking breach, though it took every drop of his will power to do so. She was so hot, so inviting; the constriction on his cock drove him to the brink of madness. After remaining absolutely still to allow her to adjust to him, he moved deliberately, gentle motions of thrusting and pulling. Soon her arms wrapped around him, and he could see the tension on her face relax.

And Torin was correct, Caitrin understood in their frenzy. The first thrust of his was nearly unbearable. Then his lips and tongue and words washed over her, a cooling loch of tender endearments, and the pain of first love slowly dispersed. When he resumed his movements, though she had to adjust to the strange sensation of her husband inside her body, she adjusted quickly — her body knew what to do and how to respond, even if she didn't. Then the pain was gone and all that lingered was the passionate intimacy of her husband making them one, and the sensations that rose from his efforts.

In his own ecstasy, Torin wasn't going to last long, that he knew. From the moment he entered her, he wanted to rush, ride her fast and come hard, but what manner of husband would he be then? Keeping his wits about him as best he could, he thrust little by little, attempting to be as gentle with her as possible. But even the slow movements couldn't suppress his raging need that built to its height.

He gazed down at her, the delicate features of her face tightened with passion, her blonde hair an inviting, golden splash on the coverlet. She was as much of a treasure in his bed as without, and the vision of her underneath him was his undoing. He lost himself in her and called out her name before collapsing on his elbows so as not to crush her.

Caitrin was still, her mind trying to resolve her actions with her husband to her usually innocent nature. In one day, she went from a virginal would-be nun to a wedded and bedded bride. She wasn't sure what to make if it all, or of this particularly gentle giant breathing heavily atop her.

He could have been quick, taken her roughly, done his duty. Instead, he spent most of his night making her ready, having her trust in his movements, soothing her in the sight of his gigantic body. What manner of man was this rough Highland warrior? Torin surprised her at every turn, and she wasn't accustomed to surprises.

She felt him stir on her chest, and a hint of a smile tugged at her cheeks.

"So 'tis how ye would woo me?" she asked with a touch of humor. Torin's body vibrated as he chuckled.

"Aye," his voice was muffled in her hair. "How did I do?"

"Weel, I think, had ye wooed me properly, ye would have achieved your goal."

"Ahh," he breathed, lifting his head to peer down at her lovely face, "I would have had ye in my bed then."

"If nay that, then at least I would have considered your marriage suit. Ye woo quite well, Torin."

He rolled to his side, keeping her encircled in his strong arms as he did. He had her now, and he was not about to let her go. That such a treasure should be his was still an unbelievable reality. He kissed the top of her head as they nestled together in the bedding.

"Weel, dinna let anyone else ken. They see me as a Goliath, the walking embodiment of the Highland warrior. If they ken I am more of a lover than a fighter, I will nigh live it down."

Caitrin sighed, relishing the touch of his fingers as he stroked her face and upper arm.

"Your secret is safe with me."

Chapter Nine: Unwelcome News Calls for a Celebration

DECLAN MACCOLLOUGH DIDN'T bother knocking on his tackman's door at sunrise the next morning. Rather, he kicked the door in, uprooting it from the metal hinges that held the door in place. As it dangled, resembling a sapling after a storm, Declan marched over the threshold.

Torin had been expecting his laird, and his anger. Emerging from behind the hanging sheet, Torin patiently wrapped a plaid around his waist and faced Declan. The bored expression never left his eyes as he regarded the shorter man.

Lady Elayne ran up behind Declan, catching herself just before she crashed into her husband. She cut her silver eyes to Torin.

"I told ye I would have to tell him," her wry tone matched her eyes. "I waited as long as I could."

Declan sputtered as his wife spoke, his face hard and cold. He was rarely at a loss for words, but the conniving between his wife, his sister, and his oldest friend was just too much. His face was hardened stone as he spoke.

"Torin! Did ye think ye could keep such a transgression from me?" Declan's wide hazel eyes burned with an angry fire. Torin could only think of one other time such anger burned Declan — that reason being the Lady Elayne, presently standing behind the Laird.

Shaking his head, Torin made a clicking sound with his tongue. "'Tis no' as much as that," he began.

"'Tis betrayal!" Declan growled, his voice lowering. "'Tis *treason*!"

"Nay," Torin countered, brushing at the thick hair that furred his chest, like he was plucking away a small pest. "She was no' promised to anyone. Weel, until the eve 'afore last. Then she was promised to me."

His matter-of-fact tone left no room for argument, and that would have been the case with any lesser man than Declan.

"The King needed her hand! He needs alliances if he's to make a united Scotland—" Declan hissed.

"Nay, he said he *may* need her hand, if she were still available—"

Too late Torin realized the error of his words as Elayne cupped her face in her palm. Declan would demand to know how they knew the King's words from a private conversation. The Laird's eyes narrowed.

"How did ye ken Robert's words?"

There 'twas. Torin's face flashed desperation to Elayne, who only pursed her lips and shrugged. Clearly, they could not give up Kaleigh, whose only thought was to do good and help her Lady and friend.

"The walls have more ears than ye ken, Laird," Torin sidestepped the question. "Your voice is loud when ye are in your cups, and many heard the King's need for barter."

Declan looked stricken at Torin's tactless words, and had Declan been a different man, he would have clutched his chest at the insult.

Torin didn't let him speak. "And ye heard Robert's dictate – she was only promised if she were not wed, or betrothed. At this, ye can speak the truth. That ye would offer your sister to help form an alliance for Scotland, but ye didna ken the lass was spoken for, by me. Tell the King we hid the truth from you as we feared ye would no' permit the lass to wed a lowly tacksman. 'Tis an oft-told tale, aye?"

Declan shook his head at their audacity, their treachery. Torin moved forward and enclosed his chieftain in a hug that dwarfed the shocked man. Thumping him heartily on the back, enough to make Declan's spine ache, Torin's tone changed.

"Congratulate me, my Laird, for I have taken a bride!"

Taking her cue, Elayne grasped Declan's elbow, gently tugging him toward the fractured door.

"Come, husband. Let us break our fast, then we shall have an announcement for the clan and make a wedding feast. Ye can have a conference with King Robert 'afore we share the joyous news."

Declan paused for a moment, considering his options. Committed to the side of valor, he allowed his wife to pull him from Torin's crushing embrace. Edging past the door, he turned to Torin, that flashing anger returning.

"We will break our fast, then I will see ye and my sister in my study. I will have her words on this 'afore I engage in any conversation with the King." His tone left no room for argument.

Torin nodded once, and from his lowered lids, watched his Laird return to the keep.

He let a long breath escape, surprised that he had been holding his breath at all. 'Twas not worry for his own skin that weighed on him — he encountered many larger and more fearsome than his own Laird. 'Twas Caitrin who caused him concern. While Torin could withstand any retribution Declan or the King doled out, he feared what they would say or do to her, or worse, that they would declare the marriage void, have it annulled, and take Caitrin from him. He had lost a wife once; he didn't believe he would survive the loss of Caitrin.

Yanking the door upright and bolting it into place, Torin heard a rustling behind the thin curtain, and a disheveled blonde head peeked around the edge. Her bright golden eyes were wide with fear and, Torin believed, a touch of panic. Now that her brother knew, 'twas a matter of time before the King knew as well.

Torin's mind spun as he drew the curtain to the side and settled his gaze on his skittish new wife. Truly, 'twas Declan who worried Torin the most. 'Twas taboo to many kinsmen to wed a close friend's sister without his knowledge or consent.

"Did ye hear him?" Torin asked, perching on the edge of the bedding.

Caitrin sat up tall, a wool tartan held against her pert breasts. Even after last night, she still retained her modesty, and her attempts to hide herself brought a grin to Torin's lips.

"He seems to think the King will be truly affronted." She bit her lip at the idea of treason against the King. Would they all hang for their actions under the cover of the last night?

"Nay, I dinna think 'tis the King who will be upset. I ken Declan. He's more injured than anyone by our plan. He's protective of ye, aye?"

She nodded, her hair spilling before her eyes. Torin brushed it aside with one hesitant finger. At least this time she didn't flinch at his touch. He smiled at that progress. That smile then disappeared beneath his beard.

"We have to meet Declan soon. He wants to hear from your own lips that this was your choice. That ye are well wedded and bedded. We can attend the hall with him to break our fast, or ye can have some oats and a dry bannock with me here."

The flush of relief that passed across her face softened her fearful expression, and Torin thought that to call her a treasure was an outrage. No bonnie lass in any part of the Highlands, nor all the world, could hold a torch to Caitrin. His breathing stopped every time his eyes caught sight of her.

"A bannock and some oats would be fine." Caitrin shifted to leave the bed, but Torin held up his hand to halt her.

"I will bring ye your meal."

His hidden smile returned, and Caitrin didn't have to be told twice. Her eyes sparkled as she tucked the warm tartan securely around her chest, then reclined against the cushions, feeling like a spoiled queen.

Torin returned with a tray holding a rough wooden bowl of parritch and a bannock. He was not wrong, she noted duly — it was an absolutely dry, crumbly bannock, and she had to choke it down with water.

He joined her in the bed, sharing a bit of her meal and relishing the touch of her skin as she leaned against him. Having this private, quiet moment was significant, for he knew well this would be the only solitude they would share for the rest of the day.

***

Fury burned off Declan brighter than the sunlight that rose over the once-peaceful horizon. Elayne ran to keep up with his long, thunderous strides. When she finally did overtake him, she grabbed at his tunic and swung herself directly in front of him. He stopped short, his face awash in anger.

"Dinna try to placate me, Lanie," he bit out. "What ye have done, what ye and *Torin* have done —"

"What have we done, milord? What have we done but kept your beloved sister close to ye, wed her to an honest and loving man on *your* land, instead of wed to a stranger or, Lord forbid, a lowlander in a far-away clan? And if she were to leave, what do ye think your mother would have done?"

Elayne was nothing if not pragmatic, Declan had to admit. He rubbed his hand through his golden mane of hair, making it stand on end. He knew what his mother would do if Caitrin were married off to another clan.

"She would leave, aye, go with Caitrin," Elayne spoke aloud the words he didn't want to hear. "Ye would have lost your mother and your sister again! I could not see ye go through that pain."

"The King —" he tried to counter.

"Nay, 'tis no' Robert that concerns ye. 'Tis your excuse. Ye dinna want to ken that your own emotions are taking hold. 'Tis your pride, your love for your sister that infuriates ye." She reached for his hand, bringing it close to her breast.

"And 'tis understandable," she continued. "'Tis your greatest weakness, how ye feel about your family, your clan. Yet, Torin is a good man, one of the best. And he was finally able to open his heart. Can ye deny him such happiness after the pain he has known? Or your sister? Ye have seen how men react to her— only your presence has kept her safe and her purity intact. With Torin as a husband, she will nary fear that again. One look from Torin will put any man in his place."

Declan huffed and nodded — he had to agree. Even he stepped lightly around Torin when the man was hot-headed and had yet to win any fight with his bear of a kinsman.

Everything his wife claimed was true, as much as he didn't want to admit it. And 'twasn't treason. If he used Torin's story, the King would know she'd never been available for barter.

A chill danced down his spine and spun in his gut. The mere idea of his sister used as barter made him feel sick. Taking a deep breath, he stepped into his wife's embrace, drawing what he needed from her strength.

"And we can prepare a wedding feast for tonight!" she cheered, clapping as she turned and rushed toward the keep.

Aye, but ye dinna have to talk to the King. Declan sighed as he watched his wife dance off. 'Twas a conversation he must have before Torin and his sister made their way to the keep.

***

The King stood by the hearth, warming his lean backside as he stuffed his face with honeyed brown bread. A collection of important men formed a loose circle around him, commenting on the present environment in Scotland. Lairds and Highland warriors from clan Buchanan, Douglas, Cunningham, and more made jokes and gave unsolicited advice.

The last thing MacCollough wanted to do was have this discussion regarding his sister in front of the Bruce's advisers, so Declan bided his time until the King moved away from the cluster of warriors. Dread filled his every pore.

King Robert the Bruce was in high spirits, fortunately, and Declan hoped that cheer would carry through with his news. *And*, Declan told himself, *'tis no' like the King had already committed her.* Hell, Robert was deep into his cups that evening — perchance he wouldn't even recall the conversation. Oh, that fortune would smile on him that way.

"Your Grace," Declan addressed the man who wore nothing that indicated his kingship. He was truly a King of the people. "I have verra minor news, a familial congratulation if you will, I wanted to share with you."

King Robert's fluffy brown eyebrows knitted with interest. "Oh, good news, I hope?" His voice was as light as his spirits.

"For the MacColloughs, aye. We shall have a wedding feast this eve. 'Twould seem my sister has been married. To my tacksman, Torin Dunnuck."

The expression on the King's face didn't change. It seemed frozen in that interested half smile, and that reaction struck a chord of fear in Declan. But Robert's eyes darkened as he stared at him. So, the King wasn't *that* far into his cups the night he discussed Caitrin as barter. He recalled his own words about Caitrin. Declan forced himself not to squirm under Robert's scrutiny.

"Your sister," the King's voice was hard. "The beautiful flaxen-haired lass ye said was no' betrothed? That is the sister who recently wed?" A shadow passed over Robert's face, ferociously different from his typical charm.

Declan dropped his head in apology and reverence. "I did no' ken her intention or their interest in each other. 'Twould seem something that grew suddenly from their interactions in the stables where Torin works and Caitrin oft, weel, hides. They forged this union yestereve, without my knowledge or consent. I only learned of it early this morning.

As soon as I confirmed the union, I came here to ye, to inform ye of the change in my sister's, uh, availability."

Declan waited, his breath catching like thorny barbs in his chest. Seconds wore on like hours.

Then a sharp clap on his back knocked him forward, shocking him to the core. Those dark shadows in the King's eyes departed just as they filled with mirth. The king was laughing – laughing at him!

"Weel, 'twould seem your sister is just as conniving as your wife can be. She and Torin out foxed us both. I may need the man on my council!" The King slapped Declan's back again. "Congratulations are in order, I would think?"

Declan took a few deep breaths before speaking, grateful for his good fortune. King Robert may be disappointed, 'twas more than evident, but he was not the sort to take his aggressions out on his people. He wasn't English, after all. A true Scotsman, he shifted his plans when necessary, and Declan realized the man was already reconsidering how to form alliances. And, Declan was now in the King's debt, as the Bruce was also sure to know. Dread filled him from toe to scalp. Declan would now be one of the King's closest and most trusted advisers, since he would probably call in that favor soon.

"My wife had a hand in the wedding, that I weel know," Declan admitted, feeling full honesty was required. "They would no' have been capable of pulling it off had she no' had a hand. She was the one who informed me this morn. I apologize if any plans for clan alliances —" King Robert held up a finger to him.

"Nay, she was no' promised to anyone. I had only just thought of it when I met her. Ye did no' ken of her interest in your man. 'Tis how life is sometimes. But now!" The King lifted his hand high above his head and addressed those in the hall, "my faithful countrymen, 'twould seem we are to feast tonight! My good friend, MacCollough, his sister has been wed to the mighty Torin Dunnuck. Tonight, we celebrate their union!"

Cheers and jeering abounded, echoing from the stones of the hall, but Declan didn't miss the grumbling from some. The Lady Elayne and Torin were correct — the lass was desired and keeping her safe with Torin may have been the best option.

Before the king stepped away, he grabbed Declan in a hug around his neck and pressed his face close to Declan's ear.

"Make certain your wife does no' interfere with any future lasses' wedding plans."

Robert's voice was light, almost mocking, but the underlying threat was not lost on Declan. He bowed to his King as the revered man returned to his advisers.

Chapter Ten: Into the Lowlands

ELAYNE WAS ECSTATIC at word from her husband that they were still in the King's good graces. Her shrewd understanding of politics told her they would be —King Robert needed more allies than enemies, and the loss of a potential bride is little concern in the larger game of Kings. She clapped her hands together like a wee bairn and raced about the keep, giving directions and commands in anticipation of the wedding festival that evening. Her shining eyes and matching smirk mocked Declan most of the day.

And she told Kaleigh to let Duncan know their names were not mentioned to the King in any way. They were blameless, and Elayne would keep it so.

Torin and Caitrin entered the keep mid-morning, just as the bustling for the celebration began. Happy nods and large grins welcomed the couple, unnerving Caitrin who all but hid behind her immense man of a husband. Torin kept a hand on her elbow, a delicate dance of support and restraint. Though they had spent the night together, her skittishness returned with the morning sun.

She may be reticent with him — Torin expected it — but to see her still try to hide in the shadows pained him. Would she ever trust the world around her?

Declan's hooded eyes met Torin's ecstatic face, and he nodded at his new good-brother. Torin returned the gesture and escorted Caitrin to her brother's study.

Declan stood at the narrow window, pale morning light highlighting the strain of the past fortnight on his harried face.

"The King won't hang us for treason," Declan announced as they entered.

Caitrin's knees buckled and she fell against Torin. The past several nights had involved more machinations than she had encountered in her entire sheltered life. If this were life with her Highland kin, perchance 'twas too much for her. But with Torin's trunk-like arm around her shoulders, the prospect of being forgiven by the King after disobeying her brother seemed much less daunting.

"Weel, I canna say I am surprised," Torin interjected. "As Lady Elayne told us last night, 'twas no' as if the lass were betrothed."

Declan turned his shoulders, his profile outlined against the stone wall. "Nay, 'twould have been another matter altogether. Though, Torin, we shall have a private discussion later."

One tawny eyebrow rose with the comment. Torin inclined his head in response. He would have to take a beating, for the first time ever, from his friend and chieftain. With the delicate Caitrin as his bride, he would welcome the skamash.

'Twould also make Declan feel better about his sister's marriage, Torin presumed.

MacCollough finally faced the couple, his hazel gaze matching his sister's.

"And ye, Caitrin, ye fully agree to this? This man, he is what ye want?" Declan flicked his thumb at Torin, who grumbled at the lowly implication.

For a moment, Caitrin held her tongue. How did she answer such a question? What she had wanted for so long was peace and quiet, mayhap to enter a convent or live far from others for that peace. Instead, she was thrust into a large Highland clan she didn't know she had and wedded the largest man she had ever seen to stay with them. What did she want? Again, the weight of Torin's arm gave her the response she required.

"Aye," she said, her voice wavering just a bit. "Aye, my brother, I swear to ye, this is what I want." And in her heart, she told herself 'twas the truth.

Declan moved to his sister, embracing her awkwardly under Torin's scowl, then punched the giant on his shoulder.

"Weel, that is good. Elayne wants a feast for ye, aye? In celebration of the nuptials. 'Twould be uncomfortable to host such an event if the bride was no' a happy participant." Declan flicked his eyes to the hall. "Ye should go find her, probably in our chamber? She wants ye outfit ye for this event. What with the King in attendance."

Caitrin paled. She had struggled enough at wearing finery for the vows the night before. What could she possibly wear for a celebration in front of the entire clan with the King of Scotland in attendance?

***

Torin and Declan left to rejoin the King in his plotting as Caitrin approached the narrow stone stairs with despair. To be put on display for King and kin? This feast was not what she anticipated when Torin put forth this mad solution.

Her mother, Elayne, Kaleigh, and several maids of the clan bustled in and out of the Lady's chambers, carrying gowns, kirtles, lace, shoes — 'twas as though all the merchants of the Highlands were displaying their wares in the keep. Caitrin tugged at her plain woolen skirt in her nervous tic before peeking her head around the doorway.

"Caitrin!" Davina cried, sighting that familiar thatch of blonde hair near the door. She dragged her daughter into the room. Caitrin's eyes were wide with curiosity and surprise. The room brimmed with crushed velvet, fur, plaid, and glinted with gold and silver. *Why all the finery?*

"We need to find ye the best gown we can," Davina explained, reading her daughter's face. Caitrin had no guile, Davina knew. Every emotion showed on her beautiful features. Caressing the soft fabric of a mossy-green gown draped over Elayne's rich bedding, Caitrin's confused gaze moved to her mother's.

"But, I have a gown. I wore a fine yellow gown last night, with the most dainty gold ribbons . . ." Her voice trailed off as Davina shook her head.

"My dearie, that gown may have worked well enough for a secret midnight wedding," Davina clicked her tongue, "but no' enough for a wedding celebration with the King of Scotland. Lady Elayne is searching the castle and has had kinsmen and women scouring the merchants for the finest lace and jewels. Many Highland Lairds, and some of their women who have traveled with them, will be in attendance. She wants ye to look the part of the sister of the Laird."

Caitrin kept her attention on the gowns spread across the bed. "Appearances are important to them, aye?" Her finger reached up to the dun-colored kerchief she regularly wore to cover her strikingly abundant hair.

"From what I have heard in the clan, both the Lady Elayne and your brother have had to overcome a sour reputation, and they do take pride in that effort." Davina stepped up next to her daughter, placing her arm around the lassie's waist. "Can ye help them keep that pride this day? Just for one day?"

Caitrin didn't have time to answer as Lady Elayne entered, nearly squealing with unnatural excitement. The normally tempered woman was euphoric working with Kaleigh to carry in a heavy, shimmering, deep-red gown.

"This!" Elayne's excitement was infections, and Caitrin reached out to touch the glory of scarlet that was the gown. "'Tis long enough, I am certain. And the separate sleeved surcoat can be removed. The high collar of the coat and deep red will flatter your lovely neck and coloring. And the low cut of the gown will flatter your shape, no' that ye need any help."

"'Tisn't real gold thread?" Caitrin asked in a hesitant, awed voice. The gold and silver touches made the gown shimmer in the light, from the sleeveless bodice to the waves of skirting, making the red appear even deeper. Indeed, she was not fit to wear such a luxurious gown. 'Twas beyond fine, and all eyes would fall upon her if she wore it.

"Aye!" Elayne confirmed. "Let us select the jewels and shoes that will best fit ye with this gown. Oh, the King himself will wish he could have wed ye yestereve!"

Caitrin cringed at Elayne's taunt. The reminder of her willful disobedience stilled her even as the rest of the women laughed and fawned over the gown.

"Torin will nay believe the bride he has wed. We must check in the kitchens and ensure the foodstuffs for this evening are underway. Ye shall rest, wash, and prepare yourself for the celebration."

As usual, Elayne's commands were followed without question. Kaleigh and several other women raced off to ensure the preparations were well underway.

***

Caitrin indulged in a warm bath, with scented soaps, and had never felt so spoiled. To take an entire day to prepare for what amounted to a supper, instead of working, scrubbing, and cooking, seemed like such a waste. But Elayne and her mother forced her to indulge this day, a celebration just for her and Torin. Not for the first time, Caitrin marveled at the events unfolding before her eyes.

Once she rose from the bath and wrapped herself in a long cotton cloth, her mother sat Caitrin on a stool and brushed her hair over and over until it shined to rival a loch at sunrise. Elayne marched in with ribbons and gems (*gems!*) for her hair and a thin underskirt to wear beneath the gown.

The light outside the window dimmed as they finished dressing Caitrin, a job that required three women. The crimson gown fit perfectly, with the front lacing up just beneath her breasts, pushing them up in gentle swells against the gown, her décolletage milky and inviting. The deeper red velvet surcoat kept her décolletage exposed, but fit tight against her neck and tapered into sharp points at her wrists. With a flip of her thumb, the coat would come undone, and she could slip it off if she desired. 'Twas a gown worthy of a queen.

The over-skirt flared out just enough to show off her slender waist, and as she moved, the gold and silver threads reflected the light, creating a dancing glow on the gown. 'Twas magical, as though the gown was crafted by fairies. The gems in her hair, pulled up in a complicated braid with a few wavy locks escaping, were almost as rich and shimmery as her hair. The effect made her hair look as if Caitrin wore a gold crown and veil.

When she rose from the stool after the women's ministrations, Davina, Elayne, and Kaleigh gasped in unison. Davina's hand flew to her mouth, and Elayne, surprisingly, was speechless.

Caitrin was striking; they knew that to be true. Even King Robert had commented on her appearance, one she tried so desperately to hide. But in this gown, with her hair so intricately coiffed, her beauty bordered on sublime. If rumors of her comeliness had not traveled the length of Scotland yet, they would by this time tomorrow.

Elayne finally found her voice. "Come, my lassie. Your husband awaits in Declan's study. Ye are to wait until everyone is seated, then enter. Your brother has arranged for a piper, so wait until ye hear his song." She leaned close to Caitrin, pressing a soft kiss on her good-sister's cheek. "Ye are divine, Caitrin, and Torin will no' regret the day he wed ye. I doubt his eyes will move from your form at all this eve," she whispered.

A soft blush pinked her cheeks, and if they thought that Caitrin could not get any more stunning, they were wrong. Elayne escorted Caitrin to the study and departed to find her own husband.

Torin tested the sturdiness of Declan's desk, resting on the edge as he waited for Caitrin. The whole event was so different from his handfast with Janet, or even the wedding he would have had with her — little fanfare and assuredly no King in attendance. His nerves shook more than he ever recalled. At least keeping his hands flat on the desk prevented them from trembling.

And that instability in his wame knocked his breath from him when Caitrin stepped through the doorway. In her deep red gown, she seemed an impossible creature, a vision from a dream. Torin rose from the desk, staring agape like a wee lad.

While he stood before Caitrin to stare at her, speechless, Caitrin took the moment to admire her husband. His own attired form was far beyond his clean tunic and trews from the night before. The dark tunic that stretched over his broad chest was velvet, rich and flattering to his russet beard and hair. Instead of rough trews, he wore lighter wool braies gathered at the knee, showcasing his well-muscled legs encased in fine leather boots. His tartan looked new, finely edged and draped across his chest and over his hips, and made him appear even larger. His wedding costume gave him a regal air, so contrary to the rough, bearish man he was known as. He, too, was a vision to Caitrin.

Torin noted her eying him and paused a moment longer, letting her eyes linger, and bowed respectfully when her nervous, golden-doe eyes returned to his face. He gifted her a small smile from under his thick beard, hoping to ease her worried nature, and extended his elbow.

"Milady," his heavy voice was low and respectful. "Ye are a vision from heaven. I am honored to be your husband and sit by your side at this feast."

Caitrin blushed from her décolletage to her hairline and curtsied, then threaded her slender arm through his.

"My pleasure, milord," she returned.

Torin shifted his head close to her ear, his bushy beard tickling her face. "Are ye ready for this, Cait? 'Tis no' too late to run off. We can hide in the cottage."

The deep rumbling of his voice vibrated through her chest, and she caught herself smiling at his effort to put her at ease. She tipped her profile to him.

"Ooch, that we could. But the Lady Elayne has put on such a feast for us, I fear 'twould be an insult."

"Aye, Cait, ye have the right of it. We will have to suffer through this feast together."

Caitrin inhaled against the tight bindings of the red gown, biting back her laughter and preparing to walk to the hall where she and her new husband would be celebrated. Grateful Torin was by her side, she was again amazed at the trust she put into the giant standing next to her.

Ducking slightly to lead Caitrin into the great hall, the echoes of cheering and calls of "huzzah" threatened to bring the walls down. The piper's high notes resounded, adding to the cacophony, and Caitrin kept her eyes forward, focusing on her chair, trying to shut out the crowd and their noise.

Torin placed her before her seat, and with an unexpected move, pressed his lips to hers, kissing her in full view of those gathered for the feast. If her blush increased any more, she would burst into flames right there in the hall.

Torin's kiss was followed by a powerful hug from her brother and a set of kisses on each cheek from Elayne. The cheering of the crowd died down as King Robert the Bruce stepped forward from his seat of honor next to Torin, taking Caitrin's hands in his own. The King's lips brushed against hers in a respectful kiss, eliciting more cheers from the clansmen, before he pounded Torin on the back in congratulations.

"We honor your wedding here tonight, Torin Dunnuck. The place of your wife as sister to the Laird, and your own place as his man and life-long friend demand a celebration of this caliber. It is my honor to congratulate you and attend this feast." The King swung his velvet-clad arm out to the crowd. "Ladies and gentlemen, let us celebrate the nuptials of Torin and Caitrin!"

The pipes kicked up, their long notes a prelude to another round of cheering, pounding on tables, and stomping of feet that reverberated in Caitrin's bones. She squinted against the celebratory sounds, cowering into Torin who instinctively moved his arm in front of her, a barrier to the chaos.

Once the noise calmed, Declan rose again, waving the guests to be seated and inviting them to enjoy their meal. Kitchen maids immediately wove among the tables, placing platters over-laden with mutton, venison, grouse, pickled eel and cherries, leeks, cheeses, rich breads, honey, and dried apples. The table of honor at the front of the hall partook in the specialty of the evening, Cockatrice — half a chicken sewn into half a roast suckling pig — and their mouths watered at the abundance of food.

A second round of servants followed, setting pitchers among the clansmen. Mulled wine, heather ale, and thick mead spilled across the tables and floor, with most of the drink making it into mugs and goblets that rose and fell with cheers and gulps. Even Caitrin found herself drinking her fair share of wine and smiling throughout the evening, having never celebrated like this. Torin found himself smiling back at her, exuding a combination of joy and pride.

***

'Twas late in the evening before Torin made a move to depart. Caitrin had handled the attentions well, but he sensed she was tiring. Men and women of the hall were reaching moments of ecstatic drunken stupor, and most of the food was gone — either consumed or fed to the hounds. Torin leaned across her lap to catch Declan's eye, flicking his head toward the door, a gesture not missed by the King.

The Bruce stood on slightly drunken feet and raised his goblet to garner the notice of the crowd. Declan's eyes shifted from the King to Lady Elayne, and Torin's hackles rose on his neck. Something greater was underlying this celebration.

"My faithful clansmen and women!" the King announced, sending up another round of "huzzahs" from those at the tables. "Be sure to celebrate hard and find your cups this night. I have word that the rest of the Highland Lairds are on their way here. Laird MacCollough will wait for them to arrive, then journey south to the Douglas land. He will be joining us, those Scotsmen who will leave on the morn —" at this, a round of groans greeted the King, who gave a humored grin in return. "Late morning. We shall start our journey to Carrick, my own Earldom, then onto the *Threave* keep deep in Douglas lands, with thanks ye to Black Douglas."

King Robert swept a strong hand to the black-haired man known as Black Douglas for more than just his hair. The man gave a subtle dip of his chin.

"From there, we will gather the clans and prepare our attack to oust the English from Scotland once and for all!"

The cheers for Torin and Caitlin paled compared to the shouts and accolades for the King. Many were on their feet, exuberant at the King's plans. The time was nigh to extricate the English for good.

Caitrin's eyes immediately flicked to her mother sitting at the corner of a lower table. Davina's expression was hidden by a headscarf that fell in front of her face, which was bowed low. A gentle shaking of her shoulders told Caitrin that her mother was hiding her tears from those gathered, and Caitrin knew why. Her mother had only reunited with her son the autumn prior, and now her son was going to be ripped from her arms again.

Unless Davina traveled with the men — women, wives, mothers often did this to provide cooking, laundering, nursing, and needed loving — which meant she would have to leave Caitrin here at *BlackBraes*. Once more, her mother would have to make the most gut-wrenching choice a woman could ever make.

Another thought came on the heels of her mother's conundrum — Torin, too, may be heading south soon, leaving her behind. Unless . . .

Caitrin's eyes shifted to the beast of a man who was her new husband. Typical of Torin, his face showed no emotion, buried behind the masterful, woolly beard. But she also didn't miss how his eyes softened as they looked over at her, an almost imperceptible movement under his brow. Did he know of her dilemma? Could he see her fears over losing her mother or her brother — or even her new husband?

A warm hand covered her anxious fingers in her lap. Torin's eyes faced forward — there was no indication he knew of her discontent but for his large hand trying to calm her shaking nerves.

Caitrin was not an adventurous woman — safe stone walls and interior libraries were more inviting — yet in her heart she knew she could not deny her mother her heart's desire. Caitrin's eyes followed Torin's hand up his thick arm to his stern face. She would have to put her faith once more into the mountain of a man sitting next to her. 'Twas more than he bargained for, and she could only hope he would acquiesce.

Amid the jeers and drinking in the hall, Torin and Caitrin finally took their leave, thanking the King and Laird and Lady MacCollough. Torin all but whisked Caitrin back to his cottage.

When they returned to the welcome quiet, Torin went immediately to his small table, placing a candle in the center for a touch of added light as he stoked the fire. The warm glow cast the cottage in a soft glow. Caitrin noted the differences in how Torin lived compared to other men in the clan. Most of the other men bedded down in the barn, in the corners of the keep, or in low tents on the perimeter of the bailey. They found their beds where they may, preferably the beds of wanton lasses.

Torin's home, in contrast, was neat, coupled with comforts not seen in a man's space. Collections of herbs, well-dipped candles, bowls and cutlery in neat stacks on a shelf—touches not seen without a woman's hand.

While she knew Torin had been handfast before, nearly married, with a bairn on the way, that had been seasons past. To see a rough man keep his house as his wife probably had kept it for him, tidy, with simple comforts, bespoke more about the man than most in the clan saw. To the MacColloughs, Torin was nothing more than a massive beast, a rough man who cared for the company of animals more than people.

Caitrin was discovering there was so much more to the man than his outward bearish demeanor. The night before had introduced her to the softer side of that man. The more she learned about him, the more he surprised her.

That surprise surged when she found her trunk and her few spartan belongings tucked away in Torin's home.

"Tis acceptable?" he whispered into her ear, his breath tickling against her skin.

She nodded, lifting her skirt as she touched her belongings to see if they were real: her engraved wooden pitcher and water bowl, her kerchiefs, an etched keepsake box (a generous gift from Lady Elayne who had a penchant for such trinkets), and her trunk of clothes and necessities. Her back was to Torin, but she glanced over her shoulder when he spoke.

"I didna ken if ye wanted to remain in your brother's keep, or if ye wanted to live here with me. I didna tell the servants 'nay' when they brought the items here. If ye would rather live in your chambers, I'll have everything sent back in the morn."

Caitrin didn't read people — they were oft far too complicated for her — but Torin's voice sounded heavy. Did he want her here?

"Would ye rather I left? That we lived separately?" Her voice was less than a wisp of air.

Torin lowered his head, keeping his eyes hooded. But again, she noticed the softening of his face. That fierce outer shell of a giant Highland warrior was only that — a shell. Caitrin was beginning to understand the man he truly was, with a softer, loving side, one he wasn't willing to show to the world. But he was willing to show Caitrin. Her heartbeat throbbed in her chest.

"Nay," he finally answered in a hoarse voice. "I ken ye did no' want to wed. That ye had little choice in the matter, that I was perhaps the lesser of two evils. But I—" He paused, his chest catching before he continued. He lifted his eyes to gaze into hers. 'Twas not the conversation that should be had with hidden eyes. "I care for ye, Caitrin. More than just doing ye a courtesy of marriage. Ye attracted me from the moment ye came to the keep and pulled off your hood and those golden eyes widened at your change in circumstance. I was no' in a good place and had been angry for a long time. Yet I saw ye standing there . . ."

His voice drifted off, and Caitrin understood what the fierce warrior could not bring to words. He cleared his throat, and when he continued, his voice was louder, more commanding.

"But I ken ye did no' ask for any of this. If ye want to return to the keep, then ye can go. We are well and legally wed. Ye are protected, and I will no' ask ye for anything more."

Her hand rested on the water pitcher as she kept her shining gaze on the man before her. He was giving her an out, but if she took it, she wouldn't be any better off than she'd been before. More importantly, if she left, then her mother would have to make that horrible choice of which child to follow. If she stayed with Torin, this giant man with an even larger heart, a man who had been nothing but caring, protecting her, loving her. Could she stay with this man and perchance one day love him?

She didn't need even a moment to consider.

"I would like to stay here with ye."

Torin thought his heart would burst at her answer. 'Twas a significant decision for her to make, and he would tread lightly. As they readied for bed, he helped her from her dress. Once she was comfortable in her shift under the bedding, Torin bundled several plaids on the rug covering the dirt floor. Caitrin raised one slender, tawny eyebrow in question.

"Ye may have offered to stay, but I would no' overstep my bounds with ye. I ken 'twill take time to be comfortable with me. I will return to the bed only when ye ask."

'Twas one concern she had, and his words sent a wave of relief. Though he did take his time with her the evening before, the prospect of another night under Torin's girth had troubled her thoughts. Could she take that on again? Would he be as gentle with her? New bride fears, to be sure, but valid ones. And ones that she evidently wore on her face in a grimace, for Torin saw those fears.

Caitrin nodded her appreciation and, feeling the bustle of the day and the festivities and drinking of the night in her weary bones, slipped into a deep sleep.

***

Damp winds kicked up as the night wore on, slipping past the mudded sides of the cottage to turn the warmth of the house frigid. Caitrin shivered under her coverings, waking in the dead of night. The banked fire had extinguished completely.

She stepped out of bed, sliding past the curtain intending to bring the hearth back to life. The cold of early spring seeped up from the ground — the rugs hung onto the chill, spreading it throughout the cottage and the soles of her feet.

Forgetting that Torin was asleep on the floor next to the bed, she tripped over him, landing in a solid heap on his other side. Her leg caught on his chest, and she noticed he too was shivering as he slept. Even his large frame couldn't ward off the bone-chilling damp and wind.

She re-lit the fire and banked it deep in the hearth then returned to Torin. Though he was in a heavy sleep, his body trembled in the frigid air. Caitrin rested a hand on his shoulder and shook him awake.

"Torin. Torin." She raised her voice to wake him.

Before she finished his name the second time, he was on his feet, a knife in his hand, hair wild and eyes alert.

"Are ye safe, lass? What's amiss?" His imposing form, clad in naught but a pair of low braies, pressed toward the door, ready to combat any unfortunate soul who should breach it.

Caitrin reached out for him, clasping his arm in her hand. "Nay, Torin. 'Tis naught to fear. Only the cold and damp."

Torin's face scrunched up. "Ye want me to fight the damp?" Caitrin's face burst into a sleepy-eyed smile. "Ooch, nay! What I mean is, 'tis cold. Ye were shivering."

"Aye, that I was, lass," Torin nodded. He wouldn't deny it. "What of it?"

Caitrin reached her hand out to touch his arm. "Ye should no' sleep on the floor of your own home, milord. Ye should, I mean, do ye, uh . . ." She couldn't bring herself to say the words. Torin drew up to his full height, sticking the knife into a band on his braies.

"Are ye asking me to join ye in bed, Cait?"

"Nay! Well, I mean, nay for, weel —?" Her voice squeaked. "But I canna bear to see ye shivering on the floor. Please come to bed."

Torin stepped toward her, his dark eyes roving over her curves the shift didn't hide.

"Aye, Cait. 'Tis late, to be sure, but I canna promise what may happen if I join ye in the bed."

Caitrin hesitated, taking in the significance of his words. Her slender hand flew to her neck.

"Weel, uh . . ." she stammered, then shook her head. 'Twas her husband, with whom she had lain with the night before. In her deepest heart, she wouldn't deny him.

"Come to bed."

Torin didn't need to be told twice. He grasped Caitrin around the waist, hauling her past the curtain into the bedding with him. Tucking them both beneath the heavy plaids and fur, he nestled her into his chest, curving his body around her back. One heavy arm stayed across her waist, his fingers brushing against her breast as he held her tight against his body.

"Ye have naught to fear from me this night. We will share our warmth and keep each other through until morning. Sleep Caitrin. I may no' be so accommodating on the morrow."

A wave of heat built under the coverings, a warm cocoon, and they promptly fell asleep.

Chapter Eleven: Realizations and Rough Journeys

CHURNED UP DIRT and tracks in the mud were all that remained of the Highlanders who had rallied to the Bruce's cause. Tents had been packed and carts and horses loaded with every manner of necessary items as they readied themselves for the trek south.

The lairds and Robert had come to a consensus — that the English had spent far too much time on Scottish land. Instead of allowing the English to move north, their logic was to press south, keep Longshanks and his army in England if possible, and rout any malingerers who may try to prevent the Bruce from establishing his throne.

'Twas a simple enough plan on the surface, but Torin knew differently. The English were as annoying as cockle-burrs which clung to and irritated everything they touched.

'Twould nay be such a straightforward matter to expel the parasites from Scottish lands.

MacCollough and his men were to follow the King as soon as a few remaining Highland lairds worked their way south. They were bringing their own contingents of men, and as spring was entrenched, the Bruce didn't want to wait any longer. Those northern-most Highland warriors would arrive at *BlackBraes* shortly, then MacCollough would lead the rest of the Highland army toward *Threave* keep, deep in Douglas land, near the English border. Black Douglas, his spine straight with pride and ambition, rode next to the departing King Robert and would organize the army once under the auspices of Clan Douglas.

MacCollough had already sent instructions to his men. He would not leave *BlackBraes* undefended, far to the north though 'twas. The English had managed to encroach this far in the past, and Declan left nothing to chance. Lady Elayne was to stay behind to command the keep and ensure 'twould be prepared for a productive spring. Duncan was promised as her second in command, his sword at her disposal.

Torin, however, had known from the time the King first arrived that he would go south with his Laird. Declan would no sooner leave without his horse than he would leave without Torin, the mightiest of his warriors.

Much to Torin's surprise and delight, Caitrin had informed him that she, too, was going south with the soldiers, with Torin. And while he didn't need to ask why, she shared her reasoning — to save her mam from having to part with one of her children again. In his heart of hearts, though, he also hoped she was joining him for him. While she had shared a few loving words and gestures, her timid nature also hid her feelings about him. He only hoped her emotions ran deep or would, eventually.

Still, he feared for her company. Military maneuvers, battles, rough living conditions of dirty tents in even dirtier clothes, those were no place for a fair woman. Caitrin's determination would not be dissuaded, and that sparked a touch of humor in Torin. His skittish little lassie was a force when she wanted to be. Perchance marriage would bring her out of her shell.

And he wouldn't deny her. How could he? If she asked for the stars, he would climb to the moon and retrieve them. To have the loveliest of women on this journey, his bride warming his bed, by his side? 'Twas more than he imagined when he first agreed to wed the lass.

And if she were by his side, he could keep watch over her, protect her himself. Though they were wed, Torin had yet heard comments and jeers about her, what these rough men wanted to do with her revered comeliness, and it took every bit of Torin's self-control not to pound his own kinsmen into the ground with his bare hands.

They were packing, deciding what to bring on a journey where they did not know how long they would be gone or if they were ever to return. Torin would leave with naught more than his plaid across his chest and his sword strapped to his back. Caitrin wanted to bring more — herbals and vittles and other necessities. Torin wiped his brow in dramatic relief at her efforts, joking that he fretted that she would weigh the horses down with gowns and shoes. Caitrin smirked and threw a kerchief at her husband.

Oh, that smile. 'Twas rare and when it appeared, 'twas like the clouds parted and the glory of heaven shined down on earth. His insides melted at that smile. Torin vowed to make it his life's purpose to encourage that smile every day.

The other Highland lairds and their men had arrived at *BlackBraes*, and they would leave in the next few days, joining the King and the rest of his army on Douglas land. But new men meant new threats, and Torin had cautioned Caitrin to either remain in the cottage or by Lady Elayne's side if she were at the keep.

The days passed almost in a blink as the men set up temporary tents on damp grass and mud in the bailey, eager and excited to join the Highland army against the English. Torin's own excitement grew in response. Readying oneself for battle made the blood churn and boil. Every hair stood on end and a man's cock grew hard as iron in anticipation. More than once, Torin had to turn away from Caitrin for fear he would ravage her, as heightened as he was.

After the sun had set, and they had returned from a loud supper at the keep, Torin made for the stables as Caitrin continued for the croft. They were ready to leave at first light, and Torin wanted to ensure their horses were at the ready. The few women who were accompanying the men would ride in a rickety cart behind the men, but Torin would ride his own steed and wanted to ensure all the horses were as prepared as he was.

The hour grew late — Caitrin wondered what was keeping Torin in the barn. Most likely, the MacCollough cornered him with a demand of some sort. Earlier, Caitrin had noticed her brother's skin pulled across his face, lines appeared where there'd been none, and she was worried for him. What had him so concerned? Leaving *BlackBraes* exposed? Leaving Lady Elayne? Should she be worried for him? For Torin? For her mother?

Dressed in naught but a shift and a plaid, she ventured to the stables. Torin leaned into a stall, giving adoring attention to a contented horse.

"Torin?" Her tremulous voice carried through the empty stables. Only the sounds of horses stomping and neighing broke the shadowy silence.

"Aye, lass. I am here," Torin called, moving toward her.

Caitrin yanked on the barn door to pull it shut and raised her eyes to her husband. Her face glowed, a pale moon in its own sky, and he felt his cock flex. The prospect of battle raged through him, and he was wary of getting too close to her.

"Are ye well?" she asked.

"Aye." His voice was abrupt.

"Are ye coming back this night? Ye have been in the stables awhile."

A rough grumble came from Torin. "Lass, ye dinna want to be near me now."

Those innocent golden eyes held his gaze. "I dinna understand."

Torin stepped close, so close the heat of his bare chest permeated her delicate shift. His raw power also flowed from him, but she stayed where she was.

"Battle, or the prospect of battle, brings out the worst in men. And nay just the violence, the killing, but 'tis an effect that ravages a man's better senses. Women fall under men in this state, either to their cock or their sword. And I worry for ye." His breathing was ragged, as if speaking pained him.

"Nay just for other men, but from me," he continued. "I fear for your safe keeping, but I also fear for your innocence. I want ye lassie, so badly every bone in my body aches for ye, but I made ye a vow. I willna touch ye again unless ye ask for me. And even if ye do, 'twill nay be like your wedding night. When men are randy, 'tis not sweet and soft. 'Tis heart-racing and hard, exciting yet forceful. I canna take ye like that."

The air between them was thick, weighted with the truth of Torin's words and intentions. Caitrin kept her fiery gaze on his face, their eyes searching one another for answers, for solace. Time spun out, and Torin felt his blood pound in his ears as her eyes fixed on him.

To his surprise, Caitrin lifted her hand to cup his bearded chin. Like this, Torin was fearsome — she could see the frightening Highland warrior in him. At the same time, he was right. The power he exuded made her own heart race, her own feelings rage within her, and she knew she was there to bring him release. She was his wife, and he had remained true to his vow. Could she deny him when his need, his desire, was so evident, it was painted across his face like streaks of blue woad dye?

"I am your wife," she told him with a boldness she didn't entirely feel. "Aye, ye ken. I am asking for ye."

Her final words were scarcely a sound, but 'twas all Torin needed to hear. He grabbed her, lifting her from the ground to crush against her and ravage her lips with his. The low growling in his chest grew louder as he worked her mouth, then nipped his way over her neck. Caitrin's heartbeat in a fit, her blood exploding throughout her body. Excitement, a thrilling sensation of fear and desire, filled her, and she let her head fall back as her husband consumed her.

None of the tender touches or gentle wooing of her wedding night. This time, Torin grabbed her shift, ripping it to yank her breasts free with a rough hand. His lips and tongue found her swollen nipple as he hiked her higher with his other arm. Her feet dangled, so she wrapped them around his hips to support her position, and her shift worked up past her thighs as her legs clung to his hips.

Torin took the invitation, slipping one hand under her buttocks, releasing his throbbing shaft that pulsed and begged for Caitrin's warm opening. He plunged in fast and deep, mildly surprised she should be ready for him. He didn't want to hurt her, but his need was so great it drove any rational thought from his brain. He didn't know if she cried out in pain or pleasure — he only knew he needed to take her, all of her, and find his release.

Her wedding night was butterflies and gentility. 'Twas everything a virginal bride should have on her wedding night.

Torin's aggressive attentions in the barn were a fire — a blazing, devouring fire that licked and burned — and she wanted more of it. These sensations were unlike any feelings she'd ever experienced. In her stoic, hidden world, Torin came in like a rampage, and the more he kissed, touched, and plunged within her, the more fiercely she wanted him. Her wedding night consummated the marriage, but their fiery joining in the barn bound them in a way no priest, or mere words at a wedding, never could.

Her back pressed against the wall of the stables next to the saddles and tack as Torin held her aloft. Crushed by his immense form, Caitrin felt more than heard his ragged breathing and animal grunting hot in her ear. She clung to his shoulders as he thrust and invaded and pounded. She had eventually enjoyed her bedding with Torin on their wedding night, but this, something was different. A buzzing, euphoric sensation built deep between her legs. 'Twas a churning river in a storm, building and growing with every thrust of her husband's member.

The more he drove into her, the more her own storm grew inside her, an unknowing, mind-numbing storm, spiraling from her core, up her spine, and to every appendage. Her arms and legs quivered, losing their grip, and at the last moment, she thought her body would explode and she cried out over and over in this strange ecstasy.

Then it was over, and her head fell against Torin's naked shoulder. As she struggled to regain her thoughts, Torin's own coarse voice roared in her ear, and he clenched, pressing her even more into the stone wall. Her skin scraped, but she didn't notice. Torin's culmination poured into her in a burning rush, and his immense body slumped against hers, pinning her to the wall. His strength seemed to leave him, and she hung against him, sweaty and breathless and confused at her response to her husband's ravishing.

They took several minutes to catch their breath. Torin regained his footing, shifting Caitrin in his arms, but didn't let her down. He kept her in his arms, holding her against his clammy chest, not wanting to lose this moment. That Caitrin met him with such passion, welcomed him so completely, aroused him more than he believed possible. And she took what he gave, calling out his name as she experienced the height of passion. Torin couldn't have asked for a more fervent joining from his wife.

"Ye are well, Cait?" he asked cautiously, cradling her as he rested against the wall. He prayed this coupling in the barn didn't injure her or worse, scare her away from his bed altogether. She wiped her damp hair off her forehead, exhaling in a long breath.

"Aye, I think so. I dinna ken what happened. I thought my skin would melt off my body," she murmured. "Was that supposed to happen? 'Twas no' like that on our wedding night."

Their bodies shook as Torin's chuckling vibrated them both. "Weel, that is what we hope to happen. With women, it does no' happen all the time. At least, 'tis what I have heard. And on a wedding night, for a lass's first time, 'tis different, no doubt. But after that first time, 'tis painless, and oft women can lose themselves, much like a man."

"Is that what I felt? I lost myself? Is that what happens to ye?"

Torin was silent for a moment, shifting his eyes to the far side of the stable before catching her gaze again.

"When a man, uh, finishes, aye, he loses himself." He lowered his head and kissed her cooling brow. "But with ye, wife," he told her in a hushed tone, "I lost myself the moment ye arrived at *BlackBraes*."

Caitrin had no words, but curved herself into Torin's chest, cuddling closer. 'Twas the only response he needed.

***

Threave Keep, Douglas Clan Lands, South of Galloway

The journey to *Threave* Keep was long and trying. Caitrin had not known how tired and achy her bones could be, and she had ridden for days before this venture. To be packed in a cart, like chattel with her mother and several other women, did not agree with her. She rubbed her sore backside. Royalty may ride in fancy, cushioned carriages, but not Highlanders. Expediency outweighed comfort at every turn, and she'd endured worse. She wanted to ask if she could ride her own horse, or any horse, even walk, just to relieve the misery of cart-riding.

But she didn't ask. 'Twould draw attention to herself, and she didn't want to inconvenience anyone, least of whom Torin who was still trying to get back into her brother's good graces. If she peeked around the cart-driver (not to be called a coachman by any stretch, 'twould be an insult to the man, she knew), she allowed her eyes to follow Torin who rode behind Declan, to the left, always ready to protect his Laird's weaker side.

'Twas what Torin did, she realized as she bounced about on a bruised backside in the cart — he protected the weak side of those he cared about. His Laird, of course. Even Lady Elayne. Rumors abounded that Torin had not taken to the Laird's Lady overmuch when she first arrived but took an arrow to the arm for her when under attack.

Then there was Caitrin herself. She passed the time reflecting on the different ways in which Torin had guarded her own weak sides — her skittish demeanor, her quiet spirit, her nervous constitution. Each time she needed strength or protection, he found her, stood as a wall between her and danger, came to her rescue, even gave her strength she didn't know she had.

He had spoken of how much he cared for her; indeed, there was so much more to him than he admitted, more than he showed his kinsmen. To take such risks, to stand strong for her in the face of his Laird and King, those emotions went deeper. His actions spoke his heart. And as she stared at the backside of the enormous man who seemed to crush the stalwart steed he rode, Caitrin understood what his actions were telling her. She gasped at the realization.

He loved her.

A cleansing spring rain welcomed them as they finally arrived at the Douglas keep, situated on an island on the River Dee. The men had intimated the keep was naught more than a pile of rocks — a fine tower at *Threave* was planned, but construction was lacking as of yet — and they did not misspeak. Most of the keep was built into the base of a low hill that scaled down to the grassy River Dee on its opposite side. 'Twould be a fine castle location one day, Caitrin surmised as she tightened her kerchief beneath her chin, but for now, she pitied those who lived inside. A snug tent or a dilapidated croft would suit her fine.

And a dilapidated croft 'twas, one that she would share with Torin and several other MacCollough warriors on the other side of the murky water and bogs surrounding the Douglas stronghold. Torin had arrived in advance of the cart and other non-essentials, the warriors being the only essentials.

The ground grew mucky as they closed in on the river. When the cartwheel caught for the final time, 'twas so firmly stuck in the mud that they were left with no other option. Grabbing all they could carry, the rest of the traveling party walked to their respective quarters. A young man, not yet in his full growth as a Highland warrior, helped her carry her small trunk to the croft, an endeavor in itself.

Leather and tartan-clad men, giants most of them, paraded around Douglas land with a strong sense of purpose and importance. Metal clanged against metal in the far reaches of the grasses, men practicing and honing their sword-craft. Other clansmen milled about near fire pits, eating or talking, a fevered air of anticipation swirling among them all. Caitrin was so caught up in watching that she didn't look where she was going and bumped into the Highland lad carting her trunk.

"We're here," the lad gruffed, though his wandering eyes told Caitrin he didn't mind the bump overmuch.

Caitrin nodded her thank you and stepped through the door as the lad hefted the trunk inside and departed. Pallets and satchels indicated where a smattering of men had claimed their sleeping spaces, but 'twas the space in the back corner that caught her attention. She knew at once 'twas the bedding Torin selected for them — the thin curtain of fabric separating the bed space from the rest of the room could only be Torin's doing.

Her heart melted. Even amid battle plans and war councils, of warrior men and uncivilized accommodations, Torin marked their place, making it as comfortable and private as possible for a shared cottage. She shook her head, truly pondering why this giant warrior did so much for her. Was this how all husbands behaved?

The man himself ducked to enter the tight cottage, his face brightening when he saw her by the bed. She gave him a timid smile in return.

"'Tis our space, I presume?" She gestured to the curtain as Torin moved close to her, pulling her into a light embrace.

"Aye. We must share space, what with so many men gathering. I wasna sure if ye would be comfortable here, so I also have a tent if ye want it t'be just the two of us."

Caitrin shook her head. Thick bedding and plaid coverings under an almost watertight roof were a sight better than a cold tent on the mushy ground.

"'Tis perfect." She didn't try to hide the awe in her voice.

"We shall have to share the bed," Torin explained with hesitance. "I could nay think of a reason why no —"

Caitrin lay her palm against his face, caressing where his beard thinned as it rose up his cheek, cool and comforting. She was touching him more, growing accustomed to this man, a comfort she once thought impossible.

"Nay. Ye are my husband. Of course, we should share a bed."

Torin dipped his face close to hers, his breath warm and his beard tickling. "Thank ye, Cait." Then he caught her lips in a light kiss, pressing gently, but a heated undercurrent of untapped passion, a burning fire, passed between them. Caitrin pulled her lips away and rested her kerchiefed head on his wide chest.

"Nay, thank ye, Torin. Ye do so much, and I would thank ye for all ye have done."

He didn't answer but kissed the top of her hair. He wanted to stay there, tell her he loved her, press his urgent need further, but they were interrupted as several men crashed through the door, offering jeers and suggestive comments until Caitrin blushed to the roots of her fair hairline. The men laughed as Torin swatted them away with an angry glare but a pleased smile. Torin pushed beyond his jocular kinsmen and led Caitrin to where the other women were setting up their workspaces.

Her mother was already by the campfire, busy flapping out damp clothing to hang in another croft. She and Caitrin shared a soft smile. Davina noted her daughter's flushed skin and sagely kept her mouth shut. Though the wedding was a sudden, secret event, the effect it had on her daughter was obvious. Caitrin may still be skittish, but she had a sense of satisfaction about her, and Davina was certain that Torin was the reason.

***

Caitrin spent her days with Davina and several other clanswomen, preparing food, medicines, and clothing for the upcoming skirmishes that were inevitable. She enjoyed these simple chores, mostly far from the noise and chaos of the keep, and so unlike her most recent stay at *BlackBraes.* During this same time, several Lairds and their men-at-arms met with King Robert, using the pile of rocks at the center of the *Threave* isle to share information and make their plans. 'Twas difficult to tell the difference between rumor and truth, and the King had to scheme his movements with incomplete information — an always frustrating endeavor.

Several pieces of information, however, were confirmed by different Lairds from different lands, so the Bruce took full stock in those reports. King Edward Longshanks was not in the best of health — 'twas the most consistent and favorable news King Robert could have heard. They weren't sure what that rumor meant, but as a result, the English king would surely be slow to make his own way toward Scotland. Longshanks was undoubtedly on his way, even if his health was compromised, the Scots surmised, as word of the King's return had spread like wildfire across parched grass.

"We should gain the advantage of their lack of strong leadership," Black Douglas impressed on the men. "The King's son is dragging his feet. Aye, several lords are assembling in towers and castles near the border, but only a few small contingents of armies have moved beyond the border to our lands. One cotillion is in Galloway, just to the north."

"Do we ken how many men?" Asper Sinclair asked.

"Nay, but ye need to ken, my King," Black Douglas hesitated.

"What have ye heard, Douglas?" Robert the Bruce probed.

"Those men, they are directly under the command of the Earl of Pembroke, Aymer de Valence."

The words hung heavy in the room.

"Feckin' Comyn's brother-by-law. Balliol and Longshanks supporter," Torin cursed under his breath. Though the Earl had command of the English armies in Scotland, living so close to the vile man made the clans want to rout the English villain with a staunch Highland charge and place his head on a pike.

The Bruce sent a furious glance toward Torin, then nodded in agreement. Even hearing the man's name offended Robert, and if he were a pyre, he would have burned to ash in front of his men, so fierce was his burning anger. 'Twas the same Earl who also held the Bruce's wife and daughter captive since the year before – an English lackey who stumbled his way into a position of power mostly due to his relationship with King Edward I of England, as first cousins. After nearly killing the Bruce at Methven nigh a year ago, de Valence took his position as commander of the English army seriously, forcing harsh rule on the local lowlanders.

The men attending the council could almost hear the king grind his teeth at the mention of the Earl of Pembroke. What Robert wanted more than anything was to fly across the moorland to Dumfries and slaughter the man who kidnapped, imprisoned, nay caged, his wife and daughter.

But killing the blackguard would not return his family – and this knowledge both haunted and tempered his ire. He needed to defeat the man, take down the English chokehold on Scotland, to have his family restored. And Robert would fight as long as he must, as long as his body lived, to achieve that goal. More than just the kingship of Scotland was at stake for Sir Robert the Bruce. Declan caught Torin's eye. Neither man envied the Bruce's position, and each sent up a silent prayer, thankful their women were safe by their sides.

"As is much of my own earldom of Carrick, and of Galloway under his control, without a doubt," King Robert added. "The English are well entrenched here, under de Valance. I dinna ken if they have reports of our gathering at *Threave*, and we can use our position to gain an upper hand. We ken the land better than the English."

His wizened eyes searched the men present. The King hid his emotions well, but all the men gathered were well versed in his hatred for this cousin who supported the English King and tried to kill the Bruce in a sneak attack.

"What do we ken of his command? What can we learn?" the King asked.

"We have the locals," Brodie Douglas interjected.

"Aye, that we do," Black Douglas confirmed. "The English here hold many of the strongholds. Their soldiers keep close to those strongholds but send out scouting parties of a score or more. 'Tis those contingents we must corral or avoid."

"We must track them," Robert agreed, "see what they know, where they patrol, and use the land against them. Douglas, Sinclair, find out what ye can amongst the locals. We shall use the very people and land of Scotland against the English, and this time we shall find victory."

The men bowed at the King and departed to work on their royal assignments. 'Twould take time — time they feared they may not have if de Valence knew the King was less than a day's ride away.

Chapter Twelve: The Welsh Barter

Near Galloway, Scottish Lowlands

GILLIVRY'S PLAN HAD followed a seemingly preset path, as though foretold by the heavens. Keeping his ear close to the ground, which was most easily done hopping from pub to pub as he had done for the past fortnight, Gill collected gossip and rumor as lassies collected flowers. And like a lassie, he pressed the gossip close, holding it for when it would next be needed.

In the course of his travels, he heard that Highlanders were marching south, several clans already at the Douglas lowland clan holding — a mound of rocks that Douglas kin called *Threave* Castle.

He was still in Scotland to collect more gossip, yet close enough to the English border lords to use that gossip as necessary. Perchance with his pockets full of knowledge, he could find his way into the good graces of King Edward, who may gift him a minor lordship with land and titles. *Lesser men have been rewarded with more,* Gill thought smugly.

After another cold night of sleeping in naught more than his plaid, he set off for the Douglas land with no sure intentions, except for a night with a whore to appease his manly needs. The Douglas keep, he'd learned while eavesdropping at the most recent pub, was at least another day's travel southwest. He flexed his sore legs and tired feet and readied himself for another long day of walking. What he wouldn't have given for a horse.

The village of Galloway appeared over a mucky hillcrest as the day waned, and Gill hobbled his way to the inn. Now that he was in Douglas land, just south of the Bruce lands proper, 'twould be necessary to take in his fill of ale and gossip. Perchance some English rumors spread this far into the lowlands. Gill reached into his sporran, touching the few coins he had left. Letting the silver slip through his fingers, he made his decision. A visit to the Stag Inn was worth the cost.

As he stepped into the muggy, stinky warmth of the pub, his flinty eyes adjusted to the dim interior as he surveyed the patronage. True to form, several men from local clans filled dense wooden chairs, their drunken chants, jeers, and songs threatening the balance of the beams above. A rickety stairway to his right most likely led to rented rooms, or rented women. The darkly polished bar to his right looked surprisingly clean, with freshly washed goblets lining the edge.

And fortune smiled upon him. Tucked into low chairs by the spitting hearth were a coterie of men who fancied themselves worldly merchants, or at least they appeared so — evidenced by their refined linen clothing that did little to keep them warm in the harsh Scottish weather. Smiling to himself, Gill worked his way to the stout barkeep, ordered a horrible spiced mead, and sat near the end of the bar to keep his ears open to both the Scots and the merchants. Rumors would abound.

Gillivry collected the information quickly, without discernment, and as much as he could possibly carry. Who knew which rumors would end up being the most lucrative? Posing as a traveler passing though the villages, rumors and news was plentiful, and Gill made it a point to tuck it all into his memory for safe keeping.

The most significant news he overheard from the merchants was, of course, the return of the false king Robert the Bruce and his movements among the clans. In some places, 'twas the only topic discussed. As Gill traveled closer to the English border, one name surfaced over and over — MacCollough. Gill cringed every time he heard the name. That Laird, that clan, was the reason the Rosses lost their own laird and were scrambling to find their way. And while Gill had no' agreed with Laird Ross's fevered, misconstrued plan to defeat the man who helped the Bruce escape capture, he understood what motivated the old Laird.

Gill also overheard that King Robert the Bruce had arrived at the Douglas clan lands and was installed at the *Threave* stronghold with his men— the names Black Douglas and Sinclair also crossed many tavern patrons' lips. Gill added that location to his list of potential tavern visits. As a Scot, his ability to find out information was keen — Scots tended to be overly trusting with their own kin. And Gill wanted to learn as much as possible about the pretend king's movements.

Clans were in-fighting, kings were fighting, countries were fighting. Rule under the English and the Balliols seemed the most sound, the most secure, Gill couldn't argue that. Scottish clans needed English oversight, not another hot-headed Scot as king. He had seen firsthand how ornery and disorganized the clansmen were. And he would use every weapon at his disposal to promote a unified English rule.

***

Over the course of two villages, one on the Scottish side of the border, and one on the English side, two pearls of information landed in Gill's open hands. The first had to do with a celebration of sorts. News had spread that the MacCollough's once-estranged sister, considered a singular beauty of the Highlands (nay, all of Scotland, some commented, calling her the 'Jewel of the Highlands'), had wed in a private ceremony with King Robert in attendance.

But not to another Laird or a man of power — nay! To a lowly tacksman, her brother's man. And though this man had a staunch reputation as a mighty warrior, a bear of a man, Gill surmised there had to be something more to *that* story.

Then, just as he crossed into England, another rumor caught his ear, and it didn't take a brilliant man to put those puzzle pieces together. Once Gill understood the significance of the second piece of information, he changed his direction, heading south toward Rose Castle in search of Lord de Lacy.

This second bit of rumor also had a financial aspect to it, an aspect that a broke man like Gill wouldn't pass by. Rain had ravaged the land, storming over it as the Goths had Rome. Mud and muck stuck to everything —the roads were heavily rutted with puddles, catching carts and wagons in deep, water-logged ruts. The fury of the weather didn't deter Gill from his aim, but when he encountered a squat pub and inn near the border, he had to take advantage of this

good fortune. The tavern offered shelter and warm food and drink, and nary a seat was to be found. Gill squatted on the hearth to warm himself and wait for a stew he hoped would help chase the chill from his bones.

He was shoveling the stew into his mouth and letting his eyes dance around the overstuffed room. He had seriously considered asking for a room for the night, jiggling the coins in his purse. If 'tweren't too dear, a dry room held much more appeal than a wet night in a cold plaid.

But when his eyes fell on a set of damp red cloaks hanging off the chairs of several hardy-looking men, thoughts of a dry room flew from his head. He wiped his sleeve across the stew that clung to his scruffy beard. Gill then shifted to the other side of the hearth, appearing to warm his backside, but really to listen in on what these English soldiers had to say.

At first, he only heard bits and clips. The name de Lacy was referenced several times, both with laughter then with a sense of eagerness, and the word "reward" fell from one of the soldier's lips. Gill leaned in, picking at the mud on his shoe and straining his ears to hear better.

"Oh, de Lacy is on fire. He paid the Welsh lord already! Who pays for an item not yet in his hand? The lord is a fool, but a rich fool. One who can afford to buy a limpid Scots bride, evidently."

"Aye, but is she that beautiful, really? And if she is, then a man has already bedded her, without a doubt. What woman is worth that much gold? And to give it to a Welshman?" A second soldier clicked his tongue, trying to be the voice of reason, but was drowned out by protests and drink from his fellow soldiers.

"Aye, rumors tell she is that beautiful. And she was supposedly untouched when she was wed. I've heard she was raised in a convent before working for the Welsh lordling. And that she was with her mother the entire time!" The first soldier chuckled and took a long swig from his mug before slamming it on the table. "I would be hard pressed to lose a woman like that, even if I hadn't paid a king's ransom for her."

"And he can't find her anywhere?" the second, disbelieving soldier queried.

The first soldier shook his head. "Nope. The lass and her mother disappeared from the Welshman's keep months ago, with no sign or word of either of them since."

Gill stilled his hands. His brain ached at the news, scrambling as it was to put together what he had just heard with the rumors he'd collected over the past fortnight. A beautiful lass? One worth money to wed? Recently lost? The pieces slowly snapped into place, as one reassembled a broken vase, and the image he created once the pieces were together was mind-numbing. *Ahh, this is interesting,* he said to himself as he nursed his thoughts.

Was the "Jewel" that the Scots spoke of this same woman? Gill couldn't recall if he'd heard where she'd come from, but he did know she'd only recently returned to her brother. With her mam. Apparently, she had been promised to an Englishman, but now was wed to a fierce Highland warrior sworn to her brother, and by virtue of that, to the pretending King of Scotland.

He wanted to giggle at the news. If the woman were one and the same (and how could she not be?), then Gill wanted to be the one to share the news with this Lord de Lacy. Mayhap coin would fill his purse once he spoke with this unfortunate lord.

Upon hearing that de Lacy wanted to take his grievances to the King, Gill decided to travel directly to Drumburgh tower where de Lacy was visiting. There, Gill heard, the lord awaited on the King of England and searched for his missing betrothed. A royal tower, Gill figured, would be a much warmer resting place than a noisy, bug-infested room at the tavern. And a much closer trek than Rose Castle. He rubbed his hand over his damp, brown mop of hair and slowly shifted away from the hearth and the gossiping soldiers.

Flicking a coin to the barkeep, he asked for directions to the Cambrian stronghold of Drumburgh, then flipped his hood up and raced out the door.

Chapter Thirteen: Fretful Encounters

THE SCOTS' FIRST conflict with the English was naught more than happenstance. A group of scouts moved up the River Dee, into the Bruce's lands which were now under control of the English by way of the de Valence, Earl of Pembroke. The Bruce's own rage at learning the numpty who imprisoned his family was in possession of his family lands chaffed him mercilessly, further adding to Pembroke's other transgressions. 'Twas an insult added to the injury. And an insult to Robert the Bruce was an insult to all Scots.

On the southern edge of Clatteringshaws Loch, a rustling of horses caught the Scots' attention, and the warriors blended into the moorlands and low-lying brush, using the rocks as cover. A Ferguson warrior gestured to the men that he would push forward to investigate.

What he came upon was a collection of de Valence soldiers, small in number, getting drunk around a campfire in the afternoon. Ferguson shook his head — the English were cocky, to be sure, but also not known for holding their drink. Several were half-dozing in their stained hauberks, not one sword at the ready. 'Twould be like picking low-hanging fruit. Ferguson wound his way back to his men and dipped his fingertips into the cool mud.

"Nary half a dozen, mostly drunk, many asleep," he said, painting the mud on his face. Several other men followed suit. "So much for the glory of the crown. We could pick them off 'afore they report back any of our locations. We dinna want them to ken where the Bruce is."

His fellow warriors nodded in agreement. Clenching their swords in their thick hands, heavily corded arm muscles flexed in anticipation. The Scots blended into the grass and fog, emerging upon the English, light-footed as spirits from the fairy realm. With the loch at their backs, the soldiers were trapped.

And slow to rise, for most were well in their cups and not expecting any sort of battle after so boring a day. One soldier who had been tending the horses thought quickly enough to mount and ride back toward north.

The scuffle was over as quickly as it began. Ferguson and his men leapt on the English with a roar, sword tips readily finding purchase. One Englishman after another fell to the Scots' weapons. The five soldiers who tried to fight soon lay awash in blood and dirt, while Ferguson and his men hardly broke a sweat. A MacCollough Highlander approached Ferguson, wiping English blood from his arm with his plaid.

"Should we give chase?" The MacCollough man tipped his head in the direction of the soldier on horseback who disappeared into the fog. Ferguson kicked muck at the body closest to him and spit on it. He shook his head again.

"Ooch, nay. We need to inform the Bruce of this event. The English will ken where we are now, and that we are no' going to sit back and let the English overrun Scots soil anymore. 'Twill nay be long 'afore the English begin their attacks. The Bruce will want to leverage this skirmish and work it in his favor."

The men agreed. Stepping over the fallen bodies, they worked their way through the heather bracken to the Douglas keep.

***

More and more men, Highlanders and Bruce supporters from all over Scotland made their way to *Threave*, an island of Scots reinforcement amid the swaths of English forces firmly ensconced in the Scots lowlands. By now, the English and Longshanks must know of the Scots' movements. As of yet, much to the chagrin of Robert the Bruce and his advisers, the English had been strangely absent. How could the English and their Scottish sympathizers let Robert the Bruce build his reinforcements right under their noses? The Bruce shook his head. The English were not known for their brilliance.

While Robert and his council hoped that all these Highlanders would assemble peacefully in the lowlands under the Bruce's banner, such hopes were tempered with reality. These were forceful, passionate warriors, and their behavior reflected as much.

Torin especially was worried. For the first time in years, he had someone to worry about, a woman who had his heart, even if she didn't know it. Every moment away from her, he feared for her safety. And try as he might, he didn't have the words to tell her.

Not that speaking was a pastime they shared. Since they had joined MacCollough and the King, Caitrin slipped further into herself. Torin had hoped that under the broad sky and away from the chaos of the MacCollough keep, she would shed her timid ways. Rather, her fears when she was at *BlackBraes* seemed magnified once they were in this raw land. Torin made sure to encourage her as much as he could, to be her strength when her fears ran amuck, but with so many people, and so many duties, she was oft left to her own devices.

Davina, thankfully, was there to pick up when Torin was otherwise occupied with Declan or the King. She had been even more attentive to her children since they had arrived, sensing the enormity of their cause here in the lowlands. Torin admired the woman who could be unbelievably staunch when most women would rather hide from the giant warriors stomping over the marshy land. She took on the role of chatelaine, directing what needed to be cleaned, cooked, or mended. And the woman kept a sharp eye on Caitrin.

Not that Torin blamed her. Several young Scots had tried to approach Cait, his *wife*, and express their interest. Thus far, most were rebuked and moved on to easier prey. If not a rebuke from Caitrin or her mother, then a rough growl from Torin was more than enough to encourage the over-eager lads to move on and let the lass return to her work.

Several men had strung a line between two decaying crofts to serve as a clothesline, and this is where Torin found Davina and Caitrin, both trying to dissuade a young man from pressing his advantage on Caitrin. Leaning against a cottage wall, Torin observed as the young man was sent soundly on his way by sharp words from Davina and a curt glance from Caitrin. The curt look made Torin smile. He oft wondered if she knew the strength she held deep within herself.

A dull brown kerchief covered her bright mane of hair and an unbelted tunic and heavy skirt in woody-colored wool hid the shape of her curves. Somehow, though, her beauty called out from beneath the coverings. Torin thanked the heavens daily on winning the bonnie lass that even the King himself was reputed to have coveted.

Though huddled under clothing that helped her blend in with her surroundings, much like a deer in the woods, she was still the most captivating creature Torin had encountered.

***

And the most distracting. Torin sighed as he watched the encounter between the lad and the women. If he expected his days to be boring, standing around, sparring with kin and clan, waiting for the English to remove their heads from their arses and make a move on Scottish soil, Torin was grossly mistaken. As the right hand of one of the King's closest friends and advisers, Torin found himself running errands, corralling Highlanders, and retrieving news, as though he were little more than a lowly squire.

Then, when he returned at night, slightly drunk and wanting his beautiful wife, she was already deep asleep, worn from her day of busywork and surrounded by other snoring men and women. 'Twas inappropriate, Torin believed, to wake his wife and demand husbandly attentions amid a crowd.

Thus, to find an afternoon when his efforts weren't in demand, when he could sneak away and perchance steal a moment of privacy with his wife, he was both irritated and amused to find a lowly Sinclair lad trying to press his affections. Fortunately, the lad scuttled away with no further inducement from Davina and Caitrin. Torin pushed himself off the wall and sauntered toward his wife.

"Good afternoon, Torin!" Davina greeted him with a wide smile, a striking resemblance to Declan and Caitrin's.

Torin knew he would always have a special place in the woman's heart for having wed the lass and keeping her close to home. She'd no idea, he was convinced, that he offered himself not solely out of sacrifice, but out of his own selfish desires. He lifted his paw-like hand in a wave.

"May I steal your lassie away, milady? 'Tis a fine afternoon for a stroll with one's wife."

Caitrin blushed at Torin's words, but Davina only flapped her hand. "Please. The lassie works too much as 'tis. She must spend time with her new husband."

"Mother!" Caitrin gave a low squeal at her mother's innuendo and blushed even more, her cheeks nearly as red as the infamous dress he would never forget from their wedding feast with the King.

Davina patted at Caitrin, shooing her away to join Torin. Caitrin flicked nervous eyes at her wild-looking Highlander husband who was looking all the more wild given their rustic living conditions. She dropped her laundry into the thatched basket by her feet and ducked under the clothesline.

"Dinna fash, lassie. The work will be there when ye return." Torin tugged her kerchief off her head, catching his breath as her golden mane danced around her shoulders.

"Where are we walking?"

"Anywhere ye desire. I apologize, Cait." Torin hung his head as he spoke. "I have no' been the best husband to ye since we arrived here. What with our work and sleeping arrangements . . ."

"We have obligations." She brushed off his concerns, as though being a newlywed was nothing of import.

"Aye," he agreed, then stopped and pulled her to face him, his hands grasping her chilled fingers. "But ye are the most important obligation I have. And I have nay attended it well."

Caitrin shifted her eyes from Torin. They had not shared an intimate moment since that impassioned joining in the barn, one that Caitrin struggled to recall without shame. Their behavior had bordered on wicked.

"I dinna need that attention."

But her words were a lie. Though she shocked herself at her visceral reaction to him that night in the barn, she had responded passionately to their heated intimacy and missed his attentions as her husband. Not that she'd admit it.

Torin placed a broad finger under her dainty chin, forcing her eyes to look to his. The desire in his gaze made her knees weak.

"'Tis no' just those attentions, my wife. Here with ye, holding your hands, or working by your side. Discussing matters of import, those are attentions a man and wife should share. I have nay seen a hair on ye since we arrived. I would remedy that."

"Why?" she asked. He had lain with her; they were fully wed, what further need did he have for her now?

"Cait, I —" Torin was perplexed. How could she not see his heart? "I wed ye for more than to save ye from the King's dictates. I thought ye would ken that by now?"

Caitrin's smooth brow furrowed. *Why else would he have wed her? So, he did love her!* She nodded at his question. Aye, she did have an idea.

"Ye are beautiful, aye," he answered her unspoken question. "Achingly beautiful, so stunning even the King himself would have wed ye if 'twas possible. Ye have to ken that."

Caitrin pursed her lips as she nodded again. She had been told *that* more than she cared to remember, and ofttimes men believed they could own that beauty for themselves without her assent. Surely, he didn't wed her only because of her appearance? 'Twas fleeting — any good Scotsman understood that truth.

"And ye are a hard worker."

Caitrin lifted her amber gaze at this. Too often, everyone commented on her appearance and her good works were ignored. The kingdom of heaven wasn't opening its doors for comely lassies, but for hardworking women — that she learned in the convent. And she had more faith in her industrious nature than she did in her appearance.

"A Highlander needs a strong, hale woman by his side, no' a simpering lass. Ye scoff at finery, wear plain clothes, and work from sunup 'til sundown. A hardworking wife is a much larger reward. And I watched ye, Cait, working in your brother's keep, nary asking for a thing for yourself."

Stepping closer to his impassioned form, Caitrin's own face softened, the shadow of nerves that haunted her retreating into the light of Torin's compliments. He saw her in a way she didn't believe anyone else had.

"And ye think your quiet nature is no' welcome, especially in so loud a clan like the MacColloughs. Ye have seen me. I dinna care for the noise, preferring the solitude of the barn, just as ye do. So, I would think we are well met."

Now her face was close to Torin's, so close his fluffy beard tickled her nose and cheek. Her breathing was shallow, an excited type of nervousness, and her breasts brushed against his chest at every rise.

Torin was opening to her, sharing his emotions, the same emotions she kept tightly locked away. How was it possible such a giant warrior of a man had deep feelings? And to speak them aloud? Could she possibly share her emotions with him like this one day? Her heart fluttered the more he spoke.

"And more than any of that," his voice dropped, his tone tight and almost, *could it be? Nervous?* His breath was warm on her face. "I care for ye. Deeply. When I saw ye come off that horse when ye arrived at *BlackBraes*, I felt a desire well up inside me that I had no' felt in years. And so many men wanted ye, I resigned any chance a grizzled Highlander such as I had. But ye were there at every turn and I lo—" He seemed to choke on his words. Caitrin squeezed his hands gently, encouraging him to continue.

"I love ye, Caitrin. I ken ye may no' love me, and I am no' asking ye to. But I need ye to ken that I have loved ye for a long while, and when God gifted me the moment to step in and wed ye, I began to believe in miracles again."

Caitrin didn't know how to respond. Her heart wanted to beat out of her chest, and she found it difficult to breathe. Lifting her hand to his face, she cradled his bearded cheek in her palm. The giant Highland warrior had just laid his heart bare to her, and she would hold that heart as gently as possible.

"I dinna ken love overmuch," Caitrin whispered, her voice getting lost on the spring breeze that blustered, a harbinger of impending rain after the few dry days. "I dinna ken how to love, or what to do if I feel it. But I can say that I do care for ye, Torin. Ye have done much for me, cared for me in ways I dinna ken 'afore. Ye make me feel secure when I dinna ken I could feel that way. I dinna understand love, Torin, but ye make my chest ache when ye are with me, when ye speak such words to me. And if that is love, then that is what I feel for ye."

And he would accept that from her. 'Twas all he really needed – the hope that she cared for him. The skies thundered, opening in a downpour as Torin lowered his mouth to hers, catching Caitrin's lips in a pressing yet delicate kiss that poured all the love, all the passion Torin felt into her. He wanted to ensure that she would know love, would understand it, one day – if not today.

Suddenly, she pulled her lips away. "Is this wooing, Torin?" she asked with a subtle grin. His face twisted in confusion before a creeping awareness made him chuckle.

"Aye, lassie. I guess 'tis wooing."

"Weel, then ye are verra good at it," she told him, kissing him again.

They stumbled their way under the threatening skies and sheets of rain into their shared cottage, kissing and touching each other's wet faces and dripping hair. It was their good fortune that the decrepit cottage was deserted, the clansmen otherwise occupied in the rain.

They scrambled against one another, pulling at skirts and tartans, shedding their drenched clothing as they moved to the bed. Excitement and a strange, heady heat pulsed through Caitrin as Torin's strong hands worked their way over her skin, spreading the heat over her chilled body.

He lifted the curtain that separated their bed from the rest of the world. Falling into the stack of blankets and plaids, Caitrin gazed up at Torin, who stood with the curtain draped across his head like a woman's veil. She stifled a laugh as Torin launched his gigantic, furry mass onto the bed, covering her from the elements.

His lips never halted, kissing every inch of her skin as Caitrin writhed and squirmed. Though such displays of affection seemed improper, nigh tawdry, in the daylight where anyone could interrupt, every time Cait was with her husband, nothing was more natural than his kissing her naked body. *Was this what love was? Was this what it was to be a husband and wife?*

Those thoughts flew from her head as Torin moved above her, the most heated part of him spreading her ready thighs and once again claiming her as his wife. Her mind spun out of her head and her singular focus was on the ecstasy Torin inflicted upon her body.

***

The cottage remained thankfully empty as they caught their breath. Caitrin's fair limbs entwined with Torin's hairy, heavy ones, a scratchy, worn plaid covering them both. Caitrin's head rested on Torin's chest, her hair serving as his own blonde covering, soft against his warrior-hardened skin. Again, he thanked the good Lord for finding her and claiming her as his own.

A sudden slamming caused them both to jump, and Caitrin dove under the coverings to hide her nakedness from the onslaught of whomever entered the cottage. Bawdy laughter preceded a voice that floated past the curtain and invaded their private space.

"Ooch, Torin, are ye spending the day abed? What manner of man are ye to do so? Some weak lordling? Perchance your bonnie lassie has kept your manhood —"

"Enough!" Torin roared at the teasing, causing Caitrin to burrow even farther under the tartan blankets. Mortification replaced her satisfied sensations she'd experienced moments ago with Torin. *Oh, that these men should know they had relations!*

Torin flew from the curtains in only the clothing nature graced him with at birth, his giant, hairy frame dwarfing the other men in the cottage. The darkly russet hair atop his head nigh touched the beams and spread across his whole body, and every muscle appeared flexed as he started toward the men. Caitrin peeked a cautious eye from under the bed coverings, marveling at the power and strength he exuded, even while fully naked.

John Sinclair feinted to his left, pretending to throw the curtain aside, most assuredly as a prank of youthful indiscretion. Torin didn't see it that way, instead clutching the young man's wrist in an iron grip that threatened to snap his bones. John paled at the giant towering over him. He hadn't forgotten the beating Torin administered to the Sinclair man back in the Highlands, and that was only a mock fight.

The cacophony of the room stilled, and Caitrin ventured to look around the opening in the draping fabric to see what was amiss. The silence was painful.

"Torin," Rolf Ferguson said, the only voice of reason in the room, 'twould appear. "'Tis only a prank. No man would presume to look upon your wife in bed."

Torin's rage cooled but only slightly. He threw the lad's arm down, and John stumbled to follow it.

"Ye dinna look upon a man's wife," Torin growled. "Enough of ye lackeys keep trying to impress upon her whilst I am no' here. Learn your lessons well and share the warning, else I will equip Caitrin with her own sword, and she can run ye ne'er-do-wells through herself!"

The light-hearted tone at the end of his speech elicited a sigh of relief from those in the cottage, John most especially. Torin was justified in his anger, they would well admit. Too many lads, and indeed too many full-grown men, found reason to bother the lass whenever opportunity presented, her fierce mother notwithstanding. The men feared Davina would run them through more swiftly than Torin ever could.

John Sinclair clapped Torin on his broad, naked back, his jocular attitude returning before it even fully left. He held no ill-will against the Highland giant.

"Get ye clothes on, ye giant love-sick fool. I hate to tear ye away from your wife," John wagged his eyebrows toward the curtain, "but the Bruce and his advisers have news to share and the MacCollough wants ye there."

John winked at Torin as he turned to leave. The men filed out, and Torin pulled on his trews and yanked a tunic over his head. Throwing a plaid around his shoulders, he glanced at Caitrin, still in her state of undress behind the curtain.

"I have to go, Cait."

"Love-sick?" Her voice was barely above a whisper, flattered that others could see the same emotions Torin had shared with her. Torin's pale, bearded cheeks sprung a color akin to sunset, and Caitrin hid her condescending smile with her hand. He bowed his head.

"Milady, I must leave."

His furry head burst through the curtain. Caitrin pulled back in surprise, but Torin was still able to reach her and planted a rough kiss on her lips before racing out into the pouring rain.

Chapter Fourteen: The Misguided Lord de Lacy

GILL'S OWN JOURNEY took him beyond the English border, across the River Eden to a crumbling structure surrounded by loitering soldiers clad in hauberks and mail. The entire area was one of laziness and drunkenness. For a stronghold so close to the border of Scotland, where the self-declared King Bruce was supposedly making his stand, the soldiers under Sheriff Sir Robert le Brun seemed unconcerned with any potential combat. Truthfully, to Gillivry, they were more concerned about their next drink or wanton woman than with war. Gill shook his head with disappointed pity.

De Lacy was rumored to be staying at or near Drumburgh hall tower, and once Gill had reposed and filled his gullet with cold English vittles, he began to ask about de Lacy. He was certain the lord wouldn't be too difficult to find, what with the reward he offered.

And Gill was correct. The tavern keeper where he found his food and drink pointed to a squat, crumbling outbuilding adjacent to the tower, shrugging off Gill as he did so. Evidently, Gill surmised, the man had fielded several such inquiries. Grinning to himself, Gill stepped out of the tavern, confident only he had the knowledge for which the lord de Lacy searched.

Gill waited in the narrow hall of the outbuilding. He was unimpressed with the tower, the crumbling structure where the king was scheduled to visit. 'Twas apparent Earl de Lucy fancied himself a true peer of the realm, a favorite of the king, a true patriot, but his present accommodations didn't show it. Gill wondered if de Lacy's actual home at Rose Castle reflected the rumored amount he paid for a coveted Scottish lass. This sorry excuse for a stronghold certainly didn't reflect any measure of wealth.

He was listening to the echoes of military maneuvers in the yard when a clicking sound of fine shoes on stone announced the arrival of de Lacy. Gill braced himself. Before he'd share information regarding the MacCollough woman, he needed to make sure his instincts about the man were correct, and he hoped de Lacy was a talker.

Gill turned, expecting a foppish lord in fine hose, velvet cloaks, and bad skin. To his surprise, a hale-looking man, younger than two score but not much, stepped into the hall. His earth-toned surcoat bore no fancy accoutrements, nothing to indicate the man was a lord of the realm. Perchance rumors of his wealth were understated? A flare of anxiety flushed through Gill at the man's presence.

"What do you want, peasant?"

Ahh, there it was, the snide posturing of a spoiled lord. His finery must still be packed away. Gill bowed low out of respect and presented his recent findings.

"I have heard ye are searching for a lost betrothed? One that ye paid a high price for?"

The dusky-haired lord spit on the ground, a gooey glob landing too close to Gill's foot. Gill feinted his leg at the lord's strange reaction.

"You mean I was robbed. I have become a joke over this, a match made in good faith with a lowly Welsh lordling. Had I known he had no say in the young woman's hand . . ." He spat again. This time Gill moved his foot quickly enough.

"Can ye tell me what transpired? How did ye come to pay a dowry for a Scottish lass to a Welsh lord?" The question wasn't just to confirm Gill's suspicions — he held an honest interest in de Lacy's impulsive actions. What manner of man did such a thing?

A strange look — one of joy and pain — passed over Lord de Lacy's face. Did the man truly care for the lass? Just as quickly, the soft expression passed, and the lord's eyes hardened and focused on Gill.

"Have you seen the woman?" he asked. Gill shook his head. "Then you don't know. This woman, I've heard-tell she has been called a Scottish treasure. She is beautiful, yes. I had the good fortune of seeing her myself over a year ago when I traveled across Wales." Lord de Lacy paused and inhaled deeply. He squeezed his beak-like nose between his thumb and forefinger.

"This is not a conversation I should have standing in this crumbling hall with a stranger. Who are you to ask me all these questions?"

Gill took his own deep breath. Time to come clean. "My name is Gillivry Ross, of Clan Ross. The late Laird Ross had a measure of grief against Clan MacCollough for their part in helping the pretender Scottish king escape. I have recently learned that the MacCollough had a long-lost sister, a shockingly beautiful lass, only just returned from Wales. And when I learned of your reward for your missing betrothed, I put the two pieces together. I dinna ken for certain if she is one and the same, but for the reward ye are offering, 'twas worth the chance."

Lord de Lacy pursed lips were silent, those hard eyes taking a measure of Gill's story. He'd heard many a tale over the past fortnight, wild tales of women found by men with open palms. One man even dragged his own poor daughter to de Lacy's gate, promising 'twas the woman he sought, if only she had a bath. De Lacy sent him away with a kick to the backside.

And his reward seemed futile and inconsequential given the recent movements of the Bruce in Scotland. Who cared for a wayward betrothed when the fate of Scotland was at hand? Edward Longshanks would spit fire if he thought de Lacy's focus was on something other than conquering the Scots. But for the coin he paid . . .

Gill's words struck a chord with de Lacy. Perchance he had information de Lacy required to find his expensive betrothed.

"Come, man," de Lacy commanded. "Let's retire to my study, fill our cups, and you can tell me what information you have."

***

The study was only moderately more plush but offered a comforting fire and spiced wine — amenities lacking in the hall. The space was narrow, the writing desk pushed against the wall to make room for the chairs. De Lacy gestured to one of the empty seats, and Gill sat heavily, pressing his blue-tinged hands toward the hearth, curling his fingers. Spring may be well entrenched, going out like a lamb even, but Scotland didn't want to lose its grip on the chill and damp, and pain had settled into Gill's fingers with a vengeance.

De Lacy handed him a dented metal cup brimming with a deep red liquid. Gill downed half the cup in one gulp and wiped his face with a tattered sleeve. *Ahh, such comforts.*

"Don't get used to it," de Lacy commented, as though he could read Gill's mind while he rested against the hearth. "We are pushing farther north soon. Longshanks should arrive before the season is out, and we will begin our final assault of those rogue Scots."

Gillivry noted how the Earl cut his eyes to him, as one of those said "rogue Scots," but sagely let the implication slide.

"Including the rogue Scot ye are betrothed to?" he asked instead, knowing it was a provoking question.

Gill kept his eyes on the fire, letting the question seep into the air. He expected de Lacy to fly into a rage, but the man was a true lord, keeping his head in the face of adversity. Mayhap the lord *was* foppish? Out of all the gossip Gill acquired, very little of it addressed the man himself. The rumors singularly focused on the lass.

"Tell me, then, what you know of my betrothed, and why you think you know the whereabouts of this woman?"

Gill took another swig of his drink, gulping the fine wine as he would a watered-down mead, and cleared his throat.

"You know of the Clan Ross?" The lord nodded — Ross was a known supporter of the English claim to the Scottish throne, with weak familial relations to the Balliols. "I was his tacksman, one of them. He confided in me his ardent hatred toward the Bruce, and the men who supported him. One clan in particular, Clan MacCollough, had helped the Bruce escape after Methven, and our chieftain focused his anger on that Laird. I still dinna ken why, truly, but 'twas a way to strike back at the Bruce, and mayhap find the Bruce's location."

The fire popped, the flames mesmerizing. Gill's tale engaged de Lacy, as his search may have reached fruition by way of this menial Scotsman in his study.

"And when Ross's attempt on the MacCollough failed, I left. I retreated to family in Edinburgh, kept my head low but my ears open. 'Twas a skill I learned early on with my chieftain. When the Bruce returned, I decided to resume my support of England and Balliol's claim to the throne and worked my way south. As I did so, I collected information, any and all news, rumors, gossip that came my way. I never knew what would be the prize that brought the pretender king low."

"One piece of information I learned," Gill's voice shifted, his tone cagey, "was the MacCollough discovered last year, when his estranged mother returned, that he had a sister. Nay just a sister, but a stunningly beautiful lass, one that had men panting in their shoes. The treasure of the Highlands, I've heard her called."

De Lacy nodded, excitement spreading across his features. "Yes, that makes sense. Did you get a description?"

He would doubt the validity of the story until he confirmed the veracity of the details. The lord may be a fop, a bit senseless with his money, Gill considered, but the man wasn't a complete fool.

"Aye. Tallish, but no' too tall. Waves of blonde hair like the mane of a lion. Golden hazel eyes that catch a man's attention and does no' let go. And a fine figure, full breasts —"

"Stop," de Lacy commanded, his face pale.

This was it. Finally, real information about the girl. He was ready to throw money at the man, but an idea came to him. Here, a Scotsman was sharing this information. His loyalties to the Scottish cause seemed weak at best. Perchance this Scot could do more for him.

"How did ye get caught up with this lassie?" Gill interrupted de Lacy's thoughts, his interest in the story of the girl peaked.

He'd shared his story, now 'twas the lord's turn to trade on details. Gill knew 'twas not a new story — men bought and sold brides all the time, and not all resulted in a wedding. Could the man have paid that much? Why? Verily, an English bride would be just as accommodating?

De Lacy's body clenched as he leaned against the stone hearth, his balled fists tight against his head. He was the image of frustration.

"She is a beauty, that is true," his voice was raspy. "But she is more than that. Virginal, but also raised in a quiet, submissive convent where she and her mother helped clean in exchange for board. A change in hierarchy or funds or something of the sort at the abbey meant they had to leave, and the old Mother Superior asked a family friend in Wales to take them in. I was a guest, visiting some of my more remote lands, and Wrexham offered me shelter on a blustery night."

His voice softened as he spoke, the memory of the woman tempering the rage that had burned so ferociously.

"There is an air about her," de Lacy sounded like a lovesick pup. "She is so meek, quiet, obedient, and then to see her, a picture of womanhood, an absolute vision. And I thought she was interested in me. She catered to my every need, offering me food, wine, setting up my bath. Surely, an unwed woman such as she was looking for a match, one to raise her above her station? I inquired with Wrexham, and from his words, I surmised he was her guardian, and if I wanted to wed her, I would have to pay for that luxury. But she was everything I wanted. So, I paid and was told to return in six months' time to collect my bride. She was gone before I returned. The swindling sap didn't even have the strong sense to alert me that she had fled."

Lord de Lacy lifted his smitten face to Gill. "If you know her whereabouts, I would have you bring her to me."

Gill inhaled a harsh breath, pinching his nose before he shared his next bit of news.

"There's more."

Gill stood and faced the Earl, his eyes stern. Retrieving the lass wouldn't be as simple as de Lacy hoped.

"What more? You know her whereabouts. We can retrieve her, and I can wed her and bed her before the month is out."

Gill gave de Lacy a long, slow shake of his head. "'Twill nay be as easy as that. Rumor has it she was romantically tied to her brother's man-at-arms, and when the King returned, they were wed. The celebration, I heard, rivaled a royal reception, and the vision of the bride in a gem-encrusted red gown gave men the most licentious of visions and dreams. The pretender King, the Bruce, was even in attendance and gave his blessing to the happy couple."

De Lacy was still, behaving like he didn't hear Gill's words, until he whipped his cup into the fire where the liquid caused the flames to rage like the fury burning in de Lacy. All that money, all that effort, and for what? She had wed! His only recourse was to try to retrieve his payment from Wrexham, and Mary, Mother of God, he knew that would be a goose chase. The lordling would give him a run for the money, and recompense could take years, if he ever recovered his coin. And at the end of it all, he didn't have the one thing he really coveted — the woman.

He wanted to shake, to scream his rage, but instead he just stood too close to the fire, letting the blaze bite at his skin. How had a meek Scottish girl managed to elude him?

***

As his anger built, Lord de Lacy began to storm the small tower room, pouting and shrieking like an obstinate bairn. Not that Gill could blame the man. He, too, would be put out had he paid for a bride who no longer existed. Gillivry's conniving mind, however, never faltered during the Lord's tantrum.

"We have another option, Lord de Lacy," Gill interjected over the man's hysterics. De Lacy spun and leaned his face in close enough to touch Gill's. The lord's skin blazed red from his exertions.

"What? Wed another? To what end? I have paid Lord Wrexham for this lass. We had an agreement!" he rampaged, spittle flying from his lips.

"Aye, but the lass is only unattainable so long as she is married."

Gill wiped the droplets from his cheek as he waited for the Earl to comprehend his meaning. The Earl, however, was too far in his cups and boiling with fury to register any thoughts. Lord de Lacy glared at Gill, waiting for him to finish.

"If the lass were no' longer wed, perchance because of the death of her husband —"

Again, he let the words hang. Lord de Lacy's eyes widened as understanding washed over him. "The lass may no' be a virgin, 'tis true," Gill shrugged, stepping away from his seat, "but she is only newlywed, still young and strikingly exquisite, and still the only sister to Laird MacCollough, presently the right hand of the usurper Robert the Bruce."

Full comprehension dawned, and Lord de Lacy's whole expression shifted. He smiled fully for the first time since Gillivry had arrived and he learned of his supposed betrothed's suspicious marriage to a local tacksman, of all people.

"And you know the man? Do you know who stole my betrothed?" Lord de Lacy's voice couldn't hide his desperation, and his bony hands grasped at Gill's shoulders.

"Aye," Gill winked at the older man. "I've spent the past fortnight passing through the Scottish Lowlands, gathering information. 'Tis why I am here, to pass what knowledge I have to King Edward. Perchance I can garner even more, pass myself off as long-lost kin in support of the Bruce."

"And what good is that to me? Are you saying you have the man removed?"

Gill rubbed at his face, trying to hide the smile that tugged at his ruddy cheeks. "Mayhap I can see to that for ye, for a fee."

All the joy drained from Lord de Lacy's face, replaced with a moue of disgust. He squinted one eye at the rough man before him. "A small fee. I have already paid too much for a used wife."

Realizing that he may have pressed his luck more than he should have, Gill bowed to the Earl, who sent him away with a flap of his hand. As Gill reached the study door, de Lacy spoke again.

"I would have you move forward with your plan. I want my bride returned. I'll send word to you when we move north to begin our suppression of the Scots. I should also caution you as to your engagements with King Edward. I have heard his health is frail as he travels north to meet his army. If you have information to share with the King, it may be difficult to meet with him, should his health begin to fail. Better yet to convey such messages to me. Leave now."

So much for a warm room at the tower. Gill, though he didn't fully agree with the Earl's request to filter his news through him, recognized an ally when he saw one. He bowed once more before ducking out the doorway. The gray skies and dank mud in the yard welcomed him as he left the tower and headed to an overhang beyond the manor house where he would make camp. He decided to work his way back north, ingratiate himself with the Douglas clan and see if he could get close enough to the blonde lassie. The Earl would undoubtedly reward him well if Gill returned the woman.

As for confirmation of the frail health of the English king, Gill made sure to tuck *that* away in his mind for future use.

Chapter Fifteen: An Occasion to Celebrate

CAITRIN REDRESSED IN the sallow light of the house, pulling a wool around her head and shoulders against the biting damp. The bed had been warm and dry with Torin. The cottage, in contrast, was drafty at best, and having men traipse in and out did nothing to retain the heat. She stoked the fire to a scorching blaze to drive out the last of the chill. She had just placed a pot of broth over the chimney bar to boil when the door burst open again, this time to the tempest of her sopping-wet mother.

"Caitrin, have ye a warm dram for your mam? I am soaked to the bone!"

Giggling at her mother's tendency for hyperbole, she scooped a spoonful of the bubbling soup into a wooden bowl and handed it over.

"I dare say ye are no' soaked to the bone."

"Weel, how would ye ken, daughter, having left me in the rain to gather the laundry while ye romped in a dry bed with your man."

Caitrin blushed to the roots of her hair as her mother cackled like a fat hen.

"My heart is happy to see ye and Torin well wed." Davina patted her daughter's head. "'Twas my fiercest hope for ye." She abruptly set her bowl on the narrow shelf next to her. "Ye are well wed, are ye, daughter?"

Concern etched Davina's face sharply, like cut stone. And even if she weren't pleased with Torin, 'twould be no use to lie to her mam; Davina read her children as simply as she read a book. Caitrin's rosy cheeks reddened even more, and she bowed her head to the fire. Her slow smile caught her mother's eye.

"So, 'tis like that, Cait?"

Caitrin rocked back on her heels, soaking in the heat of the hearth.

"I dinna ken, mother. He says he loves me, but other than ye, I dinna ken what love means. And I dinna think Torin loves me as a son loves his mam or wants me to love him that way."

Davina clucked her tongue at her overly serious daughter. Most young ladies were eager, often too eager, to jump into love with a well-built, capable man. And here was Caitrin, her time in the convent and her self-imposed solitude shading her understanding and making her question what most people experienced naturally.

In moments such as these, Davina struggled to forgive herself for keeping Caitrin hidden from the world for so long. Yet, look what happened when they did return — Caitrin had to wed promptly or be sold off to the highest bidder. Davina bit at her lip — perchance she was not wrong in keeping Cait to herself for so long.

"What do ye feel when ye are with him?" Davina probed.

Caitrin rested her defined chin in her hand, staring into the fire. Picking absently at her skirt with her other hand, she spoke as openly as she could.

"I feel nervous, to be sure. Like my insides are small tufts of heather caught in a storm, and I dinna ken when the storm will end. I have that feeling even if I just see him across the room. When he looks at me, especially in that way that is so fierce, I think I should be afeared, but nay. Instead, I find myself hoping he comes closer. I feel like I'm inviting danger, then he touches me, and all those tufts in the storm want to fall to the ground and melt. I dinna ken myself when I am around him."

A shrewd smile pulled at Davina's cheeks. While her daughter may not understand those feelings, Davina knew them well enough.

"That, my lassie," Davina said with surety, "is love."

***

The incoming news was not surprising to any of the warriors gathered in the hall. The Earl of Pembroke and Longshanks' commander in Scotland, Aymer de Valence, had dispatched detachments of soldiers to search the lowlands for the Bruce. Scouts had reported that soldiers were on the move from the southeast. With a heavy hand, Black Douglas drew on the parchment with charcoal, indicating the movements of soldiers across the brackish heathland.

"Here," Black Douglas pointed with a stick at a squiggle of lines and slopes. "Glen Trool. If we can encourage the soldiers to march north, we will have dominance."

"I dinna see the advantage?" Declan MacCollough said. "What mountains are there to help ye?"

"Nay mountains," Black Douglas returned with a slick grin. He flicked his eyes to the Bruce, convinced the King would see the asset.

"The loch." Awareness dawned across the Bruce's face, and Douglas nodded.

"Aye, my King. Here is the rise in the land to the west." Black Douglas directed his explanation to MacCollough and the other Highland warriors present who did not know the lay of the lowlands. "And here is the loch, a wide loch and mucky land that makes travel difficult. Most of the wide glen through here is blocked by the loch. This path here," Douglas's stick followed a line on the parchment, "is an abutment, buttressed by the steep foothill and Loch Trool, and is the only real passage to reach Galloway. We believe 'tis most likely where Pembroke is hiding."

The warriors craned toward the parchment, studying the strategy. Understanding flashed at once with these warriors. Trapped between a loch and a rise in the landscape, the English contingents would be at a significant disadvantage. They would have to progress single file in the section of the path where it bottlenecked. 'Twould funnel the English to their demise.

If the Scottish warriors rode in from the north, blocked the exit to the south, and had men attack from the rise of the foothill as well, they could wipe out this English contingent under de Valence.

'Twould not be a huge defeat for the English but would make the mark the King needed in his country. The Scots had tried to meet the English on their terms — large armies across wide glens – and found little success. This plan, using the Scottish landscape itself to defend her from encroachment, was sound. And the time for sitting by was at an end. The hour was nigh to begin their attacks on the English and oust the parasites from their land.

The men lauded the King and Black Douglas's plan. Though battles were never guaranteed, this one appeared sound, and the men rejoiced at the opportunity to stain their swords with English blood.

They had waited far too long already.

And as Scots, the celebration for the gathering of warriors in anticipation of a great battle began the next day. Another swarm of Highlanders from the far north arrived in time to prepare for the attack on the English (most notably the MacDonalds of Glengarry, much to the King's relief), and compete in the gathering events. Whiskey and beer flowed heavier than river water, and both men and women drank with abandon.

Games and competitions followed once everyone was well inebriated. The caber toss was the most popular event, and Torin was tapped to throw for Clan MacCollough. Davina had urged Caitrin from her chores to watch and celebrate, much to Caitrin's dismay. She had protested, trying to tell her mother that the kale would not cut itself into the stew, but Davina ignored her protests and nigh carried her to the yard.

Caitrin's eyes scanned the grounds, shocked to see huge numbers of Scots in such leisure activity. The expanse of plaid and bright hair in the pale afternoon light painted the Douglas landscape in a wash of color. As her mother dragged her toward a crowd of clansmen at the far end of the grassy glen, they passed groups of men and woman cheering at a hammer toss, several men throwing axes and dirks at targets set upon haystacks, and several men in mud up to their ankles, tugging at either end of a rope thicker than her arm. Caitrin felt as though she could watch the entire day and not see everything. 'Twas unlike any event she'd seen in her whole life.

They found Torin surrounded by a half-circle of spectators, all waiting breathlessly to see if the giant could throw his log farther than the MacDonald had. Caitrin and Davina joined the crowd. Caitrin's eyes went wide with shock to hear her mother cheer on the MacCollough warrior.

He had removed his shirt and let his tartan fall about his waist. His muscle-roped chest glistened with sweat and exertion and matted with the fur that ran over the muscles and across his firm belly. His dun-colored tartan flapped in the spring breezes, brushing against his bare, trunk-like legs encased in bound leather boots. Torin, standing in the center of the crowd, resembled an ancient Scottish god — a force to be reckoned with. Caitrin didn't want to tear her heated gaze from the man. The din of the crowd fell away as she stared.

Slapping at his chest to warm his arms and ready himself, Torin squatted at one end of the log, which was nearly three times the height of a normal man and lying on the mushy ground. He had to bite back laughter — 'twould be an insult to his Douglas hosts, but this caber was naught more than a sapling. He had carried larger pieces of tree to his woodpile in the Highlands.

He flipped the caber upright then heaved it into his arms, balancing its weight in the crook of his corded neck to prevent it from falling to the side. Taking several quick, sturdy steps forward, he lunged and threw his arms well over his head. The log soared like a bird, straight up into the air.

The caber sailed well past the MacDonald log and landed with a cracking thud across the yard, standing upright for a heartbeat before falling forward in a perfect line due north of where Torin stood. No one believed his eyes, having seen a perfectly executed caber toss. Cheers erupted from the crowd and the MacDonald clasped Torin's forearm in a firm grip. He knew when he was beat.

For Torin, the toss was nothing more than what he expected. Pride beamed from Torin's eyes when he turned to find Caitrin watching him with caution-tinged joy that shone from her own golden gaze. She'd heard the rumors of Torin's strength, of his prowess as a warrior, even witnessed him send other men scrambling in the dust. Yet, to see such a visceral display of his might caused more of that nervous, internal shaking she both desired and feared.

Amid clapping and pounding on his back, Torin pushed through the celebratory crowd to Caitrin, lifted her off the ground, and crushed her lips to his. Excitement coursed through them both, and neither had a care for the teasing and taunts shouted by those gathered.

Torin set Caitrin back on earth, both in mind and body, and threaded her arm through his.

"What did ye think?" he asked, probing for compliments like a child. Caitrin turned her shining eyes up to his proud face.

"I have naught seen such a display! My mam didn't tell me, what is all this?"

"Games, lassie. When the clans come together, they want to prove which clan is the strongest, most skilled, to show the measure of a Highland warrior. If we are fortunate, we may have pipers and a wee bit of a *ceilidh*, with dancing, later."

"Why the games?" Caitrin's nervous nature of large crowds had dispersed, replaced with curiosity and excitement. Her eyes danced from one activity to the next. "Aren't we here to prepare for battle?"

"I can tell ye why tonight. For now, will ye join me this way? Several men are sparring, playing with swords is more like it," Torin joked, and Caitrin appreciated the lightness in his voice. This was not the stern, reticent Torin who oft hid in the stables. 'Twas a man certain of his power and ready to share it with her.

"Will ye practice with them?" she inquired. Torin's whole body shook with laughter.

"Nay, I will let them whack at me for a bit with their swords, then I will knock them to the ground. 'Twill nay be sparring."

He pulled her close, nuzzling her cheek with his beard. "Will ye watch me, wife?"

She almost mistook his voice for that of a young lad, not a full Highland warrior. *He wanted to show off for her.* Caitrin's smile was nearly as wide as Torin's.

"Aye. I will even cheer for ye, husband."

Torin gave her a look of mocking surprise, then his lips claimed hers again, and this time Caitrin had no regard of who may be watching. Settling her off to the side, away from the clanging and clashing of swords, he entered the center of another cheering crowd.

The other fighters, however, groaned with dismay when Torin's mammoth hand clasped a sword. To them, it looked as though he held a child's toy, and more than one man searched about for a larger weapon. A few men even grabbed maces and shields, trying to tilt the odds in their favor.

Declan was present amongst the competitors as well, his own weapon tight in his hand, and he shook his head at their efforts. He knew they wouldn't stand a chance, no matter the weapon of choice. When it came to close or hand to hand combat, no one could defeat Torin.

The first few men sprung forward in mock fighting. Torin's eyes drifted from the men to Caitrin, who flinched and covered her eyes at each clang of metal upon metal. Even in the dull spring sunlight and dressed in drab skirts, she glowed like her own star.

For such a beast as Torin was, that he had landed quite the delicate beauty gave him pause to wonder once again at what he had accomplished in this short lifetime to deserve such a treasure. Skittish as an unbroken mare, but well worth the effort. And look how far she'd come in such a short time, joyful and celebratory among throngs of people. He wouldn't have believed it.

Then Declan called to him, refocusing his attention. The MacCollough chieftain had narrowly won his round; the chagrin of a near defeat shadowed his face. And now Torin was ready to compete and make the warriors' efforts seem like child's play.

Black Douglas, cunning and light-footed, stepped forward to challenge the MacCollough giant. The crowd gasped and tittered, sharing whispers over the pairing. Caitrin caught several words and raised an eyebrow to her mother who had joined her in the crush of people.

"The Black Douglas, he is well-ken for his ability with a sword. He will nay hurt your man, that I believe, but Torin may have more of a challenge than he realizes."

Caitrin watched, riveted at the dance of swords between the two warriors. Even in a mock battle, their muscles flexed and quivered as they heaved the heavy weapons over and over. As the conflict continued, Caitrin could see what her mother had meant. Though Torin held the advantage of height and girth, it took more effort to move that mass. Meanwhile, Black Douglas appeared to be dancing at times, weaving and shifting with lithe ease.

Torin, too, noted the man's fluid movements, and readily changed his tactics. Instead of hacking with extreme force, he lowered his weapon, allowing the smaller, dark-haired Douglas man to attempt an attack. After several steps back and sideways, Douglas chased and thrust, and Torin waited as the man overextended himself. After the third feint, Torin saw his opening and lunged, catching the man low and knocking him into the muck.

Even though he had to work for it, once again Torin was victorious. This time, Caitrin didn't try to hide her smiling exuberance. She raced from her mother's side beyond the crowd to a panting, pleased Torin and threw herself into his arms. The thrill of the games she could now understand.

Watching her man win at his games was a most exciting moment. Sharing sweaty kisses with Torin in the middle of the muddy yard, she also realized that every exciting moment she'd had was because of him, and she began to welcome this frightful, exhilarating life he had introduced to her.

That night they ate half-burnt rabbit roasted over a fire, shared beer with other clansmen, sang and chanted to the pipers' music and danced under the stars. John Sinclair took to the center of several clansmen to showcase his refined sword dancing ability against the wailing of the pipers. Caitrin's eyes sparkled – she had never known such an evening and told Torin as much.

"Come, Cait. The night grows cold, and I would have ye warm my bed."

"Again?" Her eyebrows nearly flew from her face. Torin chuckled at her reaction.

"Aye, lass, if ye will have me?"

Caitrin shifted in his arms, pressing her gentle curves against his hard body.

"Aye," she told him in earnest, "I will have ye."

Torin half-ran, half-carried a squealing Caitrin back to the cottage, fortunately empty with the attractions out of doors. He slipped her under the curtain and made slow, passionate love to his wife, her cries of pleasure bringing him to his height.

When they were satiated, unclothed, and wrapped in the warmth of their loving and the coverlet, Caitrin rested her flaxen head on his chest, twisting her fingertips in his mat of chest hair. Torin followed suit, twining her gold tendrils around his fingers.

"I am glad ye shared yourself with me this night, Cait. Did the day live up to your expectations?"

"I did no' have any expectations about a day such as this!" Her clear voice shared her lingering enthusiasm. "I have never had such excitement!"

Torin kissed the top of her head and inhaled deeply, his chest making her head rise like a ship on the waves. He needed to gather his wits before he spoke again. He hated this moment, where he must rob this brilliant gem of a woman the joy she had of the day.

"'Tis good. Because I have news from the King. The English have begun movements to the north, and the men will begin tracking them to set up an ambush. We start our scouting excursions on the morrow."

Torin's news launched Caitrin's fair head from his chest, where she looked down at him with fearful eyes. His heart ached that her nervous fears could reclaim her so easily.

"On the morrow! Torin, why did ye nay tell me?"

"I just did," he deadpanned.

"Then why all the celebration?" her brow furrowed with her question. "Should ye no' have spent the day training?"

"Weel, we did. The fighting and games, 'tis a part of it. But more importantly, we needed to unify the clans, make sure that if we are to embark on this course, all the clans are in agreement. There has been much in-fighting among the clans, even the MacColloughs have had skirmishes with the MacKenzies. The games, the drinking, the pipes, they release those past disputes, and create a stronger alliance of clans. 'Tis difficult to be angry with a kinsman who is sharing your drink, aye?"

Caitrin nodded with understanding. To see so many clans celebrating together did show a unified force. "But why did ye no' tell me when ye first learned of this news?"

"I did no' tell ye earlier because, weel, your happiness was brighter than the sun on a late summer day, and I would no' ruin such a moment for ye. I wanted the happiness to last as long as it could. Happiness is a frail thing to hold onto these days, and I will help ye hold it as long as ye can."

Torin's words struck Caitrin's heart, making it surge and ache at the same time. She shifted up and placed a soft kiss on his lips.

"I do hold happiness," she whispered against his lips, "all the time I am with ye."

***

Scouts and trackers, clad in their tartans, blended into the landscape like the fog itself, searching for English movements. Torin had joined a small group heading due east, where they found nothing but marshy grasslands and rocky outcroppings. Despite that, news from other scouts welcomed them when they returned.

Scouts from Galloway rushed the main hall, disrupting a midday meal. King Robert lifted his head from a plate of haddock when Ian Stewart burst through the doors.

"My King, we have seen the movements of de Valance's troops!"

The gathered men rose in unison at the news they had been waiting for.

"Where are they?" John Sinclair asked.

"Heading north west," Ian flicked his eyes to the King. "Through Galloway."

The King shared glances with his Lairds and advisers, and a rumble of laughter bubbled up amongst them. The King slammed his hand on the table, making Ian jump.

"We kenned it." The Bruce tipped his head to Black Douglas. "Ye kenned it. We have them. They are searching for us in Galloway, thinking that I'm hiding close to my own lands. They think to bypass our men here and ambush me in Dumfries. Ooch, the English are nothing if no' predictable."

Again, the men chuckled, settling themselves to resume their meal and listen to the King's decision. An air of confidence settled in the room as King Robert spoke.

"We will strike out this afternoon, cut through the hills and reach the glen from the west. Have the men ready for battle, and we will prepare our attack then lie in wait until the contingent arrives. We will strike them down, defeat the English at their own game, and send a message to Longshanks that the Scots will bend to the English crown no longer. This will be the first blow of many."

The Bruce stabbed his knife into a small fish and flicked it into his lightly bearded mouth. The men cheered, ate, then left to prepare their warriors for their first taste of English blood.

Torin found Caitrin working alongside Davina and Black Douglas's sister, Nessie, feeding the chickens and goats. He stood back and waited a moment before approaching. When he came upon her this way, he was struck by her stunning looks and hardworking nature. To see her dressed so plainly, a stark contrast to the beauty she exuded without effort, without pretense, he thought her more beautiful, an impossible creature gifted to the world and placed into his care.

Caitrin and Davina lifted their heads at his presence, and Davina nodded politely before stepping away to join Nessie by the campfire.

Torin took the feed bag from Caitrin's hand and set it aside before taking her hands in his. Her gaze searched his face, which looked more serious than he had been as of late. Something changed, 'twas obvious from his closed expression, one she had not seen on him since before they married. Her face drained of color even before he spoke.

"News of English movements have come in," he explained. "We leave this afternoon for Galloway. I dinna ken when I will return."

Caitrin's pale skin whitened even more, going from milky to pasty. Torin placed his arm around her shoulders to support her.

"I dinna think we will be too long. A few days at most?" he tried to soothe her, but the nervous furrow of her brow had returned with a vengeance.

That spike of fear struck deeper than her skin — she shook to the very core of her bones. Over the past several weeks, she'd grown comfortable with Torin. The security she felt as his wife was unlike anything she had known. Men didn't affront her, and if they did, Torin disabused them of their advances. She shuddered at the prospect of having to shun those advances on her own once again.

"I worry for ye, Torin. I have grown to care for ye. And selfishly, I fear I may no' be strong enough to handle every concern of the world, especially outside my brother's keep, if ye are no' here." Her head hung in shame.

Torin lifted her chin so her eyes beheld his. The ferocity he exuded as his nature bore into her gaze. His voice, however, was soft and understanding.

"I ken your fears, lass. But ye are stronger than ye think. There are many ways to be strong. And ye can be safe in the knowledge that, as I have somehow managed to gain ye for my wife, I am no' going to give that up easily. 'Twould take all the powers of God himself to try to stop me from returning to ye."

Caitrin melted into his chest, his lips finding hers, sealing his promise that he would return. And her promise that she would be strong until he did so.

Torin strode off, resembling a noble ship taking sail, his tartan flapping around his broad shoulders as he disappeared into the fog of the glen. Even this far into mid-spring, the damp and chill kept the warmth of sunlight at bay and the low-lying fog swirling among the bracken on the rivers. Caitrin heard the low grumbling of the other men collecting around the Bruce, ready to make their move on the English.

She stepped around the side of the earthen stone wall of the cottage and pulled up short. Ducking back to the corner of the croft, she peeked around the wall at her mother. Nessie had moved closer to the fire, her back discretely toward Davina who was in close conversation with a large, older man Caitrin recognized as Black Douglas's uncle, Innis.

Their closeness, and the peek-a-boo smile on her mother's face told her 'twas more than just a casual conversation. Caitrin slammed her body against the wall of the cottage, the damp stone cooling her heated thoughts.

For the second time that day, Caitrin was struck by her own selfishness. Here she was perpetually concerned with herself, wanting to hide from the world under her mother's skirts, to hide in her marriage to Torin, she neglected to realize her mother may have needs of her own. Davina gave and gave to her children, particularly to Caitrin herself, never taking a moment of her own. And Caitrin didn't bother to view her mother as anything more than her mother. That she was a woman with grown children who may be lonely — Caitrin's breath caught hard in her chest. She was suddenly horrified by her own behavior, that she hadn't taken her mother into consideration amid all of her own demands.

Just how selfish am I? Caitrin lamented. *I am no better than a bairn! I need to show mother than I am strong enough without her.* Then on the tail end of that thought, *Does Declan ken?*

She had to marvel at how, even amid the preparations of battle and the precariousness of life, love still found a way to bloom. Caitrin let her whiskey-hued eyes peek around the edge of the wall again, spying as Innis reached out to touch Davina's hand, leaned in to whisper something into her ear, then departed to the far side of the campsite.

Caitrin waited until her mother stopped watching the man's exit, then stepped around the corner of the cottage as though she'd seen nothing. Still, she had to bite back a smile at her mother's flushed skin.

"Hello, mother," she greeted with high spirits. "What is left that needs be done?"

Chapter Sixteen: Glen Trool

AS A TRUE KING should, Robert the Bruce led his men, many of them the Highland warriors with Torin and Declan, on the brief journey northwest to Galloway, right up to the marshy edge of Loch Trool. From their vantage, the loch, pristine as stained glass, extended across the glen far to the east. To the west, a short step of rock and earth rose above the loch and was bordered by a jagged, hilly swell.

Once the men saw the path between the loch and the hillside, confident smiles spread amongst them. King Robert called it a "funnel of death." The men immediately recognized it as a killing field. The English would be trapped once they started across the step.

They spent the afternoon and into the evening preparing the hillside for the attack they were preparing to launch on the steps of Trool. One group of men, giants like

Torin himself, set out into the glen, wrestled the largest boulders that could be found, some as large as a man and requiring two men to push them, and wrangled them to the top of the foothill. There the stones balanced precariously, awaiting only a light push before becoming crushing weapons.

The second set of men scurried into the trees, axes at the ready to fell the longest, straightest branches. Once a collection of branches littered the ground, they carried the limbs to the top of the hill and began the arduous task of whittling them into sharp points. When they were done, the men set the freshly hewn spears between the boulders. A surprise attack from above was ready.

The weather cooperated; the dull sunlight tried to pierce the fog and keep the rain away. Though weary and worn from their preparations, the men slept little that night, anticipation of the English arriving at Glen Trool keeping them in good spirits. Some chatted, some prayed, most stared at the expansive sky above. They rose with the sun in the morn, used woad and dark clay to paint their faces, and blended into the hillside to wait.

And be bored. Torin sat next to Declan in the shade of the hill's west edge, drawing in the dirt with the tip of his dirk. They shared matching pained expressions. Could the English be slower?

"Your bride seems please with ye," Declan commented with false nonchalance, his gaze admiring the dappling light on the glen below.

Torin raised an eyebrow. Since the wedding celebration, 'twas the first time Declan had spoken to him about a subject other than their military movements with the King. He was sure that, if Declan believed he could accomplish such a feat, he would beat Torin into submission for his subterfuge in wedding Caitrin. His laird may want to engage

Torin at a battle of fists, but he would lose. Still Torin couldn't stop the smile that spread across his bearded cheeks.

"Aye, she has taken to it well enough."

"By choice?" Declan asked in that same tone, but Torin didn't miss the suggestion behind the question.

"Aye," Torin nodded. "I have made sure 'twas her choice. Every time."

Declan's lips pursed heavily, his ire at Torin's actions and the suggestion of bedding Caitrin readily apparent. Torin wasn't ashamed about his actions at all, which raised Declan's hackles more. He may have only learned of his sister in the last year, but Declan protected her just as any good brother should.

"Declan, I hope that ye consider me to be a man who would no' betray ye, who would look to help a person in need, no' take advantage of them. And ye ken my mind was no' on marriage after, weel, everything."

His Laird nodded slowly, open to hearing Torin's intentions. Declan didn't seem likely to land a surprise punch on Torin, or stab him with his dirk, so Torin continued.

"Your sister first made her mark on my heart the day she appeared," he said earnestly. "I was surprised, having no feeling since Janet's death. I tried to tuck it away, out of respect for ye. But I got to know her, grew to care for her, and when she was crying in the barn out o' fear of being wed to a stranger and sent away from ye and your mother, I had no choice. I will admit," he paused, preparing for the rise of anger his next words would undoubtedly cause. "The opportunity to wed her was fortunate for me. 'Twas no' completely selfless. But I care for her, and she is happy with me."

"Ye are telling me the truth? She is happy with ye? Nay afeared?" Declan dragged his sights to Torin, the golden gaze he shared uncannily with his sister piercing and formidable. Torin barked out a laugh.

"Perchance a wee bit at first. But she has since come to care for me as well, and she is more afeared when I am gone. The beauty is rather taken with this beast," Torin bragged to his Laird. Declan sighed heavily in resignation, then clapped his hand on that bearish shoulder. He'd hoped for a contrite response, an apology maybe? Truly, Declan didn't know what he expected.

"I have struggled with your actions since I learned of them," Declan spoke plainly. "Even my own wife was pleased, and the King dismissed your perfidy rather quickly, the Bride be praised." They both crossed themselves before Declan continued. "Yet, when I see her with ye, she shines. She tries hard to hide from the world. With ye, she can be herself, be the lass she wants to be, no' one that must hide. Ye have helped give her more of a voice, at least that is what my mother claims. For that, I canna hold your rash and lovelorn actions against ye. Life is too short to hold a grudge."

Torin clapped Declan's back in return, rocking him from his seat on the hill. "Aye, that 'tis."

Later in the day, while Declan and Torin shared dried eel and grainy bannocks, a lookout called to the King. The men dropped their food in their sporrans and stood. Every hair between them stood on end; the time to battle the English was nigh.

***

The Scottish ambush of the small English cotillion worked to force the men through the pass, placing the cocky soldiers under King Robert's thumb. The English fools pressed across the step single file. As many of the soldiers were on horseback and the step was narrow, there was little room to maneuver. They walked cock-steady and assured as only the vainglorious can, thinking they were faster and had outwitted the Scots, believing this shortcut would have them reach the Earl of Pembroke in record time.

For those who have not seen it, and especially for those who are unlucky enough to encounter it, there is nothing quite like a Highland charge to strike fear into the hearts and bowels of men. Half-naked Scottish Goliaths roaring over the side of the hill was the stuff of nightmares, and the look of shock and horror upon the English faces bespoke the nightmare they found that day.

When scouts announced the approaching English, the Highlanders took their places, ducking low at the apex of the hill, boulders and spears ready. Once the soldiers and their horses were well entrenched on the step at the narrowest point, Robert and his men gathered at the ends of the pass, closing any potential escape. Torin crouched in the sparse, rocky grass next to Declan, crazed smiles plastered on their painted faces, the air heady with breaths of anticipation. When the King gave the signal, all the warriors on the ridge rose up in unison.

Declan's skilled aim hurled sharp-tipped spears at the trapped men who scrambled to cover themselves. With their attention focused on the rain of spears, they were too distracted to protect themselves from the rush of boulders that Torin and the other bearish Highlanders rolled down the hill, crushing English legs and knocking them off horses. The sounds of breaking bones and agonizing screams echoed in the narrow pass. Soldiers spilled over the edge of the loch into the deep, sucking waters that dragged their armored weight under.

As the Englishmen scrambled along the narrow step, they only further clogged their escape and created more panicked chaos. The Scots laughed from above as they watched the English fall to such an astoundingly simple attack. Short, direct, and effective, the Scotsmen gloated.

Confusion and turmoil overwhelmed the English, announcing to the Scots 'twas time to finish raining down hell.

Broadswords and claymores drawn, the Highlanders charged over the hill in a mass of frightening-looking men, hacking and slicing at anything English they could find.

For those soldiers trapped on the step, the Highlanders made quick work of them, leaving the rest of the contingent to bleed to death on the steps of Glen Trool. 'Twas a short battle, as Robert's men outnumbered the English, at least this time. Torin lamented only one man found death under his claymore, the rest littered in blood and gore at his feet. The message, King Robert hoped, was one King Edward and Aymer de Valence would hear loudly.

Once the damage was done and the battalion dispatched, the Scots slipped back into the fog just as quietly as they had arrived, sweaty and dirty and full of pride.

While they worked their way back toward *Threave* keep, the King tempered their exultations, noting that defeating so minor a regiment was naught more than what a bairn could do.

"Aye," MacCollough echoed to Torin and several other men as they marched, their victorious faces turning more serious. "Next time, de Valence and his sheriff, le Brun, will undoubtedly bring a much larger army with more men than we have at *Threave*."

John Sinclair had joined them. The young Highlander, his face streaked with rivulets of sweat mixed with dirt, ventured his opinion, agreeing with Declan. "And we will no' have the advantage of surprise. The English ken we are here, on the offensive. Something as deceptively simple as this attack will no' suffice in the future."

The King, too, overheard Sinclair's words, nodding his head. He was beyond weary — the weight of the crown bore down in more ways than one could imagine. And if he were worn, he knew his men must be as well. They feared for their families, clans, and lands just as the King did. Perchance even more, as they had lived this English nightmare whilst he had been away.

Sinclair was right, and the King hoped MacCollough, Douglas, and Sinclair's minds could create another bout of magic for their next attack. Their strategy in the future must be near perfect.

***

News of the King's temporary encampment at *Threave* stronghold spread rapidly along the borderlands. Gillivry believed his luck would hold and that he would find the valuable woman nearby.

As a Highlander, Gill moved among the Scots with relative ease, taking on his good-brother's name of Finlay as a disguise. He blended into the background, just another Scot in support of the Bruce, and set up his own camp along the perimeter of the Douglas lands. He also feigned interest in the Bruce's movements, hoping to not only return a woman to her wealthy betrothed, but mayhap bring news to de Lacy, or even Longshanks himself. Any assistance Gill brought to King Edward would be amply rewarded, he convinced himself.

Alas, he had arrived just after the men left for Glen Trool but celebrated with the victorious Scots in their drunken antics late into the evening after they returned. Gill's celebration was not for the Scots victory over a stupid regiment of English who couldn't find their way around Scotland with a Highland scout. Instead, Gill celebrated his own success made late in the afternoon before the men returned, just as the dull sun kissed the rocky landscape to the west.

In truth, he finally understood why Lord de Lacy spent the coin he did, why he was willing to spend even more on Gill's venture, why men across the Highlands fought for her attention, and why a secret wedding.

Gill came upon the treasured lass just as she pulled the kerchief off her face. She dipped it in a pail of water and wiped at her dewy skin. Her hair formed a golden halo around her face, as though she were sent directly from the heavens. Even her whiskey colored eyes, the water of life, sparkled more than any jewel he had seen. Though a bit slender, her hips and bust swelled enticingly, and she moved with such deliberation, it seemed to be a dance.

She wore such plain, baggy clothing, evidently hiding herself, but 'twas no hiding her true loveliness. Frozen in his spot, Gill's chest caught as he stared at her, a vision in the setting sun that lit her silhouette on fire. He was completely mesmerized. For a brief moment, he wanted her; he wanted to steal her away and bury his manhood deep inside her.

Then she turned her back to him, breaking the spell. Gill slapped his hand to his face, rubbing it roughly to regain his mind. When he lifted his eyes again, she was gone.

A thrill of alarm surged through Gill, then he shook his head and wandered to where she'd stood. A few broken-down cottages and patched tents sat beyond the campfire where she had worked. Gill ambled past, appearing as nothing more than another Highlander going about his duty. A side-glance caught sight of her rough skirts as they disappeared through the rickety doorway of a cottage.

Gill kept walking, admiring the glen that extended to the southeast past the River Dee and onward to the English border beyond his view. As he continued his solitary promenade, his plan to bring the lassie back to the Englishman began to form. Gill needed to keep the bonnie lass in his sights as much as possible to make his plan come to fruition. And the Highland habit of long celebrations full of drink would help him in this endeavor.

Chapter Seventeen: An Arrow, Straight and True

CHEERING AND STOMPING announced the return of the men to the encampment, and relief flowed through the Douglas lands like a burst dam on the River Dee. Davina held back and watched as Caitrin's head lifted at the sounds of the raucous warriors, her profile barely visible as darkness claimed the land. Caitrin stiffened and dropped her bucket in the dirt. As if the night were calling to her, she lifted her stained skirts and ran with the enthusiasm of a child, full of wild abandon, in the direction of the Highland army.

Contentment surged sudden and full through Davina — her daughter, while she may have had to wed in haste, was truly satisfied in her marriage to the MacCollough giant.

Before the men even reached the Douglas stronghold, drink appeared in their hands, splashing from one cup to the next. Torin shared his own cup with Declan, handing it off when Caitrin materialized, a bright star in the dark, running to him at full speed.

Torin caught her as she leapt into his waiting arms, kissing him fully, grateful for his return. She pulled her strength from him as she pulled his tongue from between his lips. Desire, mixed with relief and anticipation, swirled in her head and spread to her chest and belly. Torin clasped her close, ignoring the whistles and jeers of his kinsmen, and carried her back to their croft. She didn't know if he would be able to remain with her, but she didn't care. She seized this moment with him, here and now, and she wasn't about to let go.

Declan and several men continued to hoot at the display as they left, but Torin's strong legs never faltered as he took his bride to their bed.

"I canna stay," he told her after a short, heady moment of intimacy behind the thin barrier of the curtain. He kissed her nose, her chin, and her forehead, and she nodded in understanding.

"The men will want to celebrate with ye, aye?" Caitrin asked, pulling the plaid blanket over her breasts.

Now that his hot, furry body no longer covered hers, the night chill pricked her nipples and made her shiver. Torin helped tuck the plaid tighter against her delicate skin, kissing her shoulder before it left his view.

"Ye can come with," he invited. "Celebrate with your brother and I?"

He waggled his thick eyebrows at the invitation. Caitrin barked out a laugh.

"With all those loud men? Have ye lost your senses?"

Torin chuckled at her wide-eyed protest. Grabbing his plaid, he pulled the dark green and black around his hips and belted it. He didn't don his tunic right away; instead he returned to the bedding, bare-chested, close to Caitrin. She reached out a milky hand and threaded her fingers against his heavily furred chest. Once again, she marveled at the ease she felt with this otherwise frightening man. She'd come to enjoy Torin when he was bare like this.

"I will come back drunk, that I ken. On the morrow, the King will most likely want a feast, to mingle with his men and begin planning our next strike on the English. That, I think, will suit ye more."

"Aye, and my mother, I am certain."

Torin sat up straight at her comment, his eye narrowing. "Why will your mam feel more suited tomorrow? I expected her to accompany ye anyhow?"

A slender smile tugged at Caitrin's lips, and she covered her mouth with her hand.

"What? Is there something I dinna ken?" Now Torin's eyes were wide, wanting to gossip just like an old crone.

"I can no' say, but Innis Douglas has spent a good deal of time with my mother. I saw them standing close, verra close, together several days ago. And I would swear on Christ's Bride that I saw him touch her hand."

Torin's face hardened, absorbing Caitrin's words. "I dinna ken the man. I will talk to Declan about him. But for ye, Cait, are ye fine with this? I mean, for so long 'tis been only your mam and ye."

Caitrin shook her head, her honeyed hair spilling around her in such a way that Torin wanted to climb back into bed with her. Her slender smile remained.

"If he is a good man, then my mam deserves him. She has sacrificed her whole life for me, then more trying to come back to Declan. Now that we are both wed, secure in our positions, 'tis time for her to find her own happiness."

Flushed with pride at the strength it must have taken Caitrin to acknowledge her mother's trials and her consideration for her mother's satisfaction, Torin nodded. He kissed her hand with a gallant flourish. "I will ask about the man and let ye know if he's worthy of the MacCollough kin."

"Of *that* I have no' doubt," she answered.

***

Torin was not the only man who kept an eye on Caitrin. Other than the regular looks of appreciation from clansmen, Gillivry watched the lass as the hawk watched the rabbit. She was valuable prey he wasn't going to lose.

The husband, on the other hand, would definitely be a problem. Gill recalled the man from the year before, when the Ross clan initiated their failed attack on the MacCollough. The giant had taken an arrow to the shoulder and fell to the ground where he remained for much of the fight. Gill didn't recall seeing the man again after that moment, and he certainly didn't remember the man being such a bear. He'd heard rumors, of course, but believed them to be exaggerations.

Now that he saw the man for himself, upright on those tree trunk legs, his head reaching the stars, Gill realized just how frighteningly large the man was. Obviously, he was recovered from the arrow wound. And not only did Torin live up to the rumors, the sheer size of the man complicated Gill's plans. Gill ground his teeth together. If he wanted to remove the lass from her husband so she could again be marriageable, he had to kill the giant, and that may prove significantly more difficult than he'd anticipated.

Night had enclosed the land fully by the time Torin carried Caitrin through the door of the cottage. Unless he wanted to get caught peeking into their romantic interlude, Gill needed to find a way to pass the time until he could place Caitrin in his sights again. He was still staring at the cottage when a heavy thump of an arm landed across his back, and he stumbled forward to catch his balance.

"Finlay!" A rough, drunken voice spat into his ear, and Gill cringed away. "We are drinking in celebration of Scotland! Where is your drink?" The drunk spun around, calling out to another man in the dark. "Ferguson! Give the man some mead!"

The man's breath was enough to fell a horse, and Gill flinched his head to the side. Before he could beg off, a tankard of foam landed in his fist, while another hand shoved the mug to his face. Forced to either drink or incur the ire of drunken men, Gill took the easy way out — he drank. He figured the lass wouldn't leave the cottage again this evening, and he was not about to take down the giant amid his clansmen. For tonight, he'd set his plan aside and partake in the frivolity. A night of revelry was always a welcome distraction.

Men in every form of undress and states of drunkenness found their rest where they passed out, and rose in the morn, dirty with heads aching from too much imbibing. More than one Highlander had drenched skin and dripping hair from dunking their heads in the horse troughs to assuage their hangovers. Davina speculated that if the English ever did want to gain the upper hand against the Scots, all they must do is invade after a night of rousing. Though Caitrin laughed along with her mother, she also shushed her against saying such treason aloud.

Davina and Caitrin were not surprised when Torin showed up to the campfire near the cottage, water droplets in his hair sparkling like diamonds in the morning sun.

Just that morning, the Bruce and his advisers discussed moving farther north, chasing the English as they ran for their Scottish holdings. The time at *Threave* was coming to an end. But upcoming battles and necessary strategies with councilors must wait. The King had managed to keep his wits about him and declared the day one of celebration. Even with knowledge of the more complicated battles to come, the Bruce and his men, and the faithful in the Douglass encampment, began preparations. Though a small victory, 'twas a victory nonetheless, a much required one after the last year of bitter disappointment and defeat. 'Twas necessary to keep spirits high and retain their present momentum.

While the threat of upcoming confrontations with the English hung above their heads, the clans weren't letting that interfere with the small victories they had achieved. What was a Scottish battle without the feasting and drinking after? Now 'twas time to mark the occasion — the first success of what the King and his men believed to be many.

Several warriors scattered north, past the wet grasses of the River Dee toward the woods in search of fattening deer and rabbits. Large men had large appetites and demanded large morsels in return for their efforts. Thrush and grouse were aplenty so close to the river, which also provided ample trout and a few early salmon. Meanwhile, the women in the camps assisted the Douglas women in cleaning and preparing all manner of foodstuffs.

Torin's stomach grumbled at the prospect of such a varied sideboard, so much so that his antics regarding the upcoming celebratory evening meal was driving Davina to the brink of madness. He hadn't gone hunting with the other men, preferring to stay close to Caitrin and the other MacColloughs. In the early afternoon, after shooing Torin away from the stew pot hanging over the fire pit for the third time (though Davina felt the number was more like thirty), Davina requested that Caitrin head to the shores near the River Dee and find watercress and perchance parsley and spinach. Then she begged that Caitrin take Torin with her, as though he were naught more than a wee laddie up to his ears in antics.

Caitrin laughed heartily at her mother's request, finding it difficult to envision her beast of a husband as a wee bairn. Noting his childish behavior, she had to agree with her mother. Poor Torin needed something to do since he wasn't hunting. Having him hunt for edible greens was the answer.

Though the afternoon was bright, and mild enough for mid-April, she grabbed her brown and green plaid at the same time she retrieved her basket from the cottage. Clad in only his threadbare tunic that pulled taut against his massive chest, Torin's own tartan hung low to brush against his bare thighs. The hair on his legs fairly matched the hair on his head, and the view of those strong legs sent a thrill of excitement across Caitrin's spine. That such a warrior of a man should be her husband, a man she could rely on and who made her feel safe, and then share her bed at night, was a daily marvel.

Holding out her hand, Caitrin grasped Torin's fingers and wove her arm through his as they worked their way toward the river.

***

As Torin and Caitrin neared the water, the air cooled slightly, and the greens grew in fruitful abundance. They seemed to be the only ones from the Douglas lands to come this far, so they were alone when they reached the river tributary. They giggled like children on this errand, chasing each other through the grasses near the riverbed.

Once they reached the river, Torin waded into the shallows of the riverbank to yank up fluffy watercress and watch Caitrin as she moved among the drier grass, scanning for spinach and parsley. He was so engrossed in both his endeavors, he didn't notice anything amiss until an arrow dug deep into his lower shoulder, feeling like it struck bone.

Torin grunted in surprise, grabbed at his chest, then fell back into the shallow water with a hard splash. Caitrin turned when she heard him groan and screeched as he collapsed.

"Torin!"

She lifted her skirts and ran toward him into the icy cold shallows, only to be blocked by an unfamiliar man on a horse who splashed up from the tree line. A bow dangled in his loose grip.

"Ye can come with me peacefully, lassie," the grizzled man told her as he situated the bow around his back, "or I can make ye come with me. 'Tis your choice."

The dark-haired man touched his sword to emphasize the lengths he would go to abduct her. Caitrin's eyes widened, mind-numbing fear filling her. *Was Torin dead? Who was this man? Where did he want to take her? Where was Torin?* Then she had a moment of clarity. This strange man didn't kill her as he may have with Torin. He needed her alive. Torin's words echoed in her ears: *YE ARE STRONGER THAN YE KEN.* She took a deep breath and acted in a way she never had before — she faced the man directly and spoke.

"I will no' leave my husband." Though her voice wavered, she stood her ground. Until the man bent over in a rush, and everything went black.

The swaying of the ambling horse woke her, followed by a searing pain on the side of her head. Dampness dripped over her temple, but when she raised her hand to touch her face, her wrists caught. She looked at her lap to find her hands tied in a crude knot of rope. Realization settled in as her aching mind came into focus. She was bound, on a horse, sitting before the man who shot Torin. Whipping her head around, she hoped to see Torin following them, tracking them at least. All she received for her efforts was another piercing pain in her head.

"He's dead, I am certain," the man behind her said in a terse voice. "I watched him grab at his chest. 'Twill do ye no good to try and escape for him."

He shifted her weight in his arms, urging the horse into a gallop now that he no longer had to hold her inert form. The jouncing caused even more pounding in her head, and she struggled to keep her mind clear.

"But dinna fret," his voice lightened. "Your real husband is waiting for ye near Dumfries."

For a moment, Caitrin couldn't understand what the man was saying. *Torin was in Dumfries?* It didn't make sense.

"Lord de Lacy is waiting at the tower at Greyfriars Kirk. Ye will wed him, as he has rightfully paid for that privilege. and ye shall be Lady de Lacy. Isn't that fancy?"

Caitrin struggled to collect her thoughts. *Paid for her? Who was Lord de Lacy? How could she wed him? She was married to Torin.*

"But I'm married already . . ." she tried to explain, but the man jostled her.

"Nay, no more, I am sure. Torin fell hard under my arrow. The giant is surely bleeding to death in the shallow waters of the river."

The man's harsh words brought stinging tears to her eyes, and she blinked them back. Torin would want her to be strong in the face of this abduction. The least she could do was not become a simpering lassie. Torin was not dead, that she knew. She felt it deep in her heart — a simple arrow from such an inept excuse of a man couldn't conquer a warrior such as Torin. Caitrin kept that belief close in her heart. To believe otherwise was unthinkable.

Chapter Eighteen: Unexpected Strength

THE CHILL OF the water and the small waves that lapped at his face helped bring Torin back to reality. His left shoulder burned every time he moved it, even as he breathed, and a throbbing ache sat in the back of his head. Rising to his shaky feet, he noted the blood circling in the river and the rock that sat just under the water. He felt the back of his skull. A goodish chunk of his skin was embedded in the stone. *'Tis well I have such a thick head, as Declan has oft said.*

His eyes ached when he tried to look at his shoulder. The arrow tip that extended out of his tunic dripped with river water, and blood stained his tunic. Holding the arrowhead with his left hand, he snapped off the tip. The rest would have to stay in his shoulder until he found someone to help him extract the fletched end from the wound at his back. Then he lifted his eyes to the bracken by the riverbank.

Caitrin! She wasn't by his side, or anywhere he could see. Worry threaded through his veins, colder than the river water. Near the bank, he found fresh hoof prints in the sandy mud, several smaller footprints (*Caitrin!*), and a smattering of blood in the crushed grass.

The hoof prints overlapped before fading to the east. Indecision froze him in place. His gut wanted him to race east, after his wife where the hoof prints led. But without a horse, and injured, he wouldn't stand a chance — his aching head ruled with sagacity. Resigning himself, he scrambled to the Douglas stronghold as fast as his injured arm would allow, hollering for Declan at the top of his lungs.

Black Douglas, hunting with his kinsmen, heard Torin's yells across the glen. Scanning the landscape, his eyes found the huge man running awkwardly, holding his shoulder, and Douglas raced to his aid. He yelled to a clansman nearby to rush to the MacCollough, then yanked his tartan from his chest and wrapped Torin's bloody arm against his torso.

They lurched their way to the campsite, only to be met by Declan, John Sinclair, and several Douglas clansmen on fresh horses. Davina's fair head peeked from behind one rider.

"Torin! What has happened? Where is Caitrin?" The Douglas man helped Davina off the horse. Clutching her basket, she bent to Torin where he reclined on the ground and poked miserably at his wound.

"I'm fine. 'Tis a flesh wound at best. A rider on a horse took her and headed east. We must retrieve her now."

He remained stoic at Davina's ministrations, not even flinching as she and Declan forced the arrow past the bone and out the back of his shoulder. She stuck her finger in the hole, feeling the damage the arrow had done. Torin was fortunate that the arrow was not aimed even a fingertip lower, or 'twould have caused a more serious injury, one the giant would not have walked away from. The heat Davina felt on his skin was not from pus — that was also fortunate, but from a simmering anger and fear for his wife's safety.

Davina scrubbed the hole in his upper arm, a clean shot they could see once the arrow was removed, and packed it with her poultice. Using clean strips of linen, she wrapped his shoulder and upper arm, then tugged his tunic back over his shoulder. She wanted to tell him not to use the arm, but she knew her words would fall on deaf ears. The giant was already discussing with Declan how to track and retrieve Caitrin. He wasn't going to sit behind to nurse his arm.

"Why was she taken?" Declan asked. *In retribution against the MacColloughs? For what reason?*

"MacCollough, I have heard rumors," John Sinclair, always a man with his ear to the ground, spoke up. "Rumors of a beautiful woman and the English lord searching for her."

"What rumors?" Declan and Torin shared a confused glance. How did they miss a rumor about Caitrin?

"Her name wasn't mentioned. Only that a most comely lass, considered the gem of the north, was supposedly purchased from a Welsh lord as a bride, but she went missing before he could wed her. I only just now put the pieces together."

Declan cut his eyes to Davina. "Did ye ken such a thing? Was Caitrin betrothed?"

Davina's face was pale and horrified. "Nay! Wrexham was no' her guardian or in any position to offer her for marriage. The lowly lordling was most likely trying to exploit our situation. 'Tis a blessing the message about ye came to me when it did, or your sister may already be an English bride."

"She may well be one now, if they believe Torin to be dead, and if not, what with their secret wedding, the English may well claim they were nay married a'tall." Declan pursed his lips at the thought of Caitrin at the mercy of the bloody English.

Another Douglas jumped down from his horse, setting the reins in Torin's good hand. Several broadswords were packed on the animal, ready for Torin's selection. Davina had remounted behind the Douglas man. Her fierce gaze shifted from Declan to Torin.

"Find my daughter. Bring her home to us."

The men rode off in a burst of dust and fury, the warmth of the day adding to the fire of their anger. They pushed the horses to their limit, the tracker on the lead horse finding evidence of the stranger's horse with ease.

"See the deep hoof prints? More than one rider on the horse, and 'tis no' moving fast. A slow gallop at best." He pointed to the swath of trampled grass as they rode.

When they approached Dumfries, Black Douglas noted where the tracks were leading and realized where the English lord had probably welcomed Caitrin.

"Greyfriars Kirk. 'Tis little more than a crumbling stack of rock and dirt. But if I wanted to wed an unagreeable woman quickly, those premises are English and accommodating to unwilling brides."

Douglas flicked a dark glance at Torin and changed his tone. "Not that the wedding would be legal, regardless, her husband presently riding to the Kirk and all."

The men fell silent, as a wedding was the least of Torin's worries. De Lacy might try to press his rights as a supposed husband, or worse, kill the lass should she reject him, and this worry spurned the men to ride across the lowlands as though they chased the devil.

And perchance, in a way, they did.

***

The sun was low in the western sky by the time the strange man arrived at a ramshackle building on the outskirts of Dumfries. It loomed like a slumping stone monolith set on drawing Caitrin into its long shadows and never releasing her.

As they approached, her mind continued to spin. She had found such happiness with Torin as of late, a contentedness, a peace she didn't know was possible. He loved her, guarded her, and her own heart fluttered whenever she caught sight of him. 'Twas during this miserable, fearful ride that she realized how much she had come to care for the beast. Her life shattered when she saw his bloody body fall into the river. 'Twas then she realized she loved him, and now she agonized that she may have lost her chance to tell him so. She bit back tears that he died not knowing her love.

The stranger dismounted, throwing the reins over the iron hitching post and hauled Caitrin off the horse. Her head no longer throbbed, thankfully, but the blood on her face itched and blinking did nothing to dislodge the dried flecks that collected on her lashes. What pained her more was the creeping horror over what was going to happen to her.

Dim firelight welcomed them as the stranger dragged her into a short hall at the base of the crumbling tower adjacent to the church. A bony, refined man in a dark blue velvet surcoat rose from the chaise by the fire and received them with open arms.

"Gill! Ye have done what ye promised!"

The cheer in his voice dropped when he saw the blood on Caitrin's face. The man, whom she presumed to be the Lord de Lacy the stranger had spoken of, gripped her chin to take in the injury. She yanked her head back with a defiance she didn't know she had.

"What's this, Gill?" Pretension tinted de Lacy's every mannerism, sickening Caitrin. He was everything her strong, warrior husband was not. Just thinking of Torin made her cringe inwardly. "I told you to bring her to me unhurt."

Gill shoved Caitrin into the hall, where she stumbled into the Earl's arms.

"She did no' want to come. She needed some, uh, encouragement."

De Lacy's lips curled with ire, and he dismissed Gill to tend to Caitrin.

"Come with me, milady. Let's get ye cleaned up."

Gill cleared his throat. De Lacy merely glanced over his shoulder at the errant Scot. "Wait for me here. Let me care for her, and you will have your renumeration soon enough." De Lacy sat Caitrin on the threadbare chaise, then stepped up to Gill. "And the husband, he is dead, correct? I want nothing to interfere with this wedding. I have paid more than enough as it is." De Lacy's forceful words left Gill no other option of responding.

"Aye. The man is dead. Give me my coin, wed the lass, and start your legacy."

De Lacy gave Gill a nod and returned to Caitrin. Gillivry exited to wait on the steps of the kirk. The lord's wedding most assuredly would happen later this evening, and Gill was not going to depart until he had coin in hand. He had time — he could wait.

"Here, milady."

De Lacy had retrieved a bowl and a cloth from the decrepit kitchens and used the damp cloth to wipe at the blood on her face. His touch was gentle, but the presence of his fingers on her body made her skin crawl and her stomach roil.

Torin, where are you? Please come find me! she begged silently, hoping her prayer reached her husband before this man's twisted plan came to pass. Meanwhile, Caitrin's features remained hardened, her attempt to convey a courage she did not feel.

Once her face was cleaned, de Lacy untied her bound hands. She rubbed at the reddened skin while de Lacy picked at her plain, soiled skirts, and *tsked* at her blood-stained kirtle. She'd lost her kerchief at one point, and her leather slippers were muddy from the river.

"In the salon through there," he pointed with one slender, pasty finger to the door near the hearth, "you will find a clean kirtle and gown more fitting to your future station as Lady de Lacy. I have a priest waiting in the sanctuary for us. As soon as you are ready, we can be wed."

Curiosity got the better of Caitrin. *Who was this man? Why did he think to wed her?*

"Who are ye? I am already wed." Again, her bold words carried on a shaky voice.

De Lacy chuckled, running a finger under her chin. "Wrexham is a vassal of mine, and when I visited my Welsh lands last year, I saw you working with that other woman. Wrexham offered your hand to me, for a price, and truth be told, I was a bit smitten. It was time for me to wed, to have a son to pass my titles to, and you are so fair, it appeared a fine proposition. I have been searching for you since you disappeared. As for your husband . . ." He waved a hand in the air. "If he's not dead yet, I am sure he will be. You are a bit stained, but I will still have you for the beauty you are."

Caitrin's chest caught and breathing became difficult. *How had this happened? Was the man mad? And what of Torin? Was he truly dead?* She thought she was becoming crazed, losing her senses, and she remained in a daze as de Lacy walked her toward the salon where her third wedding costume hung on the wall, awaiting her.

While not the stunningly red gown with the tight-sleeved coat, the blue velvet matched de Lacy's own surcoat.

The open arms were edged in white rabbit fur that tickled her nose. The shift to be worn underneath was soft and creamy on her fingertips. As a lass who regularly wore rough clothing suitable for chores, the types of dress she'd worn over the past several months were the stuff of dreams.

And though a resplendent gown all told, never would she permit that dress to grace her body. A light hand rested on her shoulder, de Lacy's hand, and she stiffened under his touch.

"Come, the priest awaits, and I want you in a wedding gown suitable for a Lady."

Caitrin leaned back, her gaze a golden sword that wanted to pierce the fool. Who was he to think she'd get dressed and join with him? A rogue stranger who had her husband killed and kidnapped her? The man's brain had to be diseased to think they would wed. She heard Torin's words in her ears again, urging her to be strong. She lifted de Lacy's hand off her shoulder and dropped it as she would offal.

"Leave your hands off me. I will no' be your bride this night. My husband yet lives, and ye should fear for your life when he finds ye here."

Lord de Lacy's face darkened, and he replaced his hand, this time clasping her arm in a painful grip that made her knees weak. Panic flared in her chest. *Can I be strong? Oh, Torin, I dinna ken if I can be this strong!*

"Get dressed. I paid for you to be Lady de Lacy. And you will be."

She thought he would leave after his proclamation — instead, he moved to the slightly ajar door and leaned against the wall to watch her dress. Caitrin was immobile, unable to take her wavering gaze from this monster of a man. *How was this happening?*

***

Declan and Torin led the charge on the kirk, raining down fury on the empty church yard.

Gill shot upright as the Highlanders drew near, his mouth hanging agape. 'Twas incomprehensible. The husband lived! That was the first impossibility Gill needed to register in his shocked mind.

The second impossibility was that the supposedly dead husband managed to gather his own forces and find their location. Gill scrambled to his feet, stumbling as he tried to climb the steps of the tower to hide.

But his disbelief slowed him, and with a peal of fear, he heard Torin's voice echoing among the stones.

"Declan, ye take the lookout. I'm for Caitrin!"

Torin leapt off his horse and flew up the steps three at a time. His large frame effortlessly burst through the weathered door, and he stormed into the decrepit hall like a conquering demi-god of yore. His mammoth body scarcely fit in the hall, his hair brushing against the sagging beams as he called forth in a thunderous voice.

"Caitrin! Where are ye lass?"

Perched on his toes and ready to attack, Torin ignored the throbbing in his shoulder, holding most of the broadsword weight with his stronger right hand. His eyes scanned the dimly lit room, searching for any sign of Caitrin.

A broken-down door near the hearth burst open, and the contemptuous English lord entered, Caitrin held before him like a shield.

Pathetic excuse for a man, Torin thought, *hiding behind a woman.* Surprisingly light-footed for a large and injured man, Torin slinked forward, his sword a frightening steel extension of his formidable arm.

"Leave the lassie, ye sorry man. Grab your sword and meet me as a man should. A true warrior will fight for his woman, no' barter for her," Torin mocked.

"You must think me a fool. You can see I am unarmed, and you are attacking an English stronghold. The army will be here soon to dispatch you."

"Ye are a fool, de Lacy," Torin spat at the man. "I ken where I am, and that army? Ye shall be waiting for a while. The Scots dispensed with an English army up in Galloway just yesterday. Ye are no' in the position ye think ye are."

"You would not attack an unarmed man who holds your woman in his hands," de Lacy challenged. A thin grin parted Torin's beard.

"'Tis exactly the man I would attack."

Torin flicked his hardened gaze at Caitrin who was visibly shaking under de Lacy's grip. He tipped his head forward, praying the lass understood the meaning of his next words. That she may be harmed otherwise sent an unfamiliar shot of fear that rocked him to his core.

"Ye dinna have the strength to fight me, de Lacy."

At Torin's words, Caitrin thrust herself to the side, trying to slip out of de Lacy's arm. She was unsuccessful but moved enough for Torin to make his attack. When de Lacy's body shifted with Caitrin's movement, he took his eyes off Torin and exposed the delicate skin and pulsing tendons of his neck.

Torin's aim was perfect. Towering over the distracted man, Torin lunged with his sword upraised. At the last second, de Lacy whirled his head, his eyes squinting at the glinting sword slanting at his head, the last image he would ever see. When the broadsword hit, the look of shock was permanently etched into de Lacy's face. The sword cleaved the Earl from his neck to his shoulder, and de Lacy's whole body when limp. Death claimed the man before he hit the stone floor.

Torin then caught Caitrin as she floundered with de Lacy's fall. Caitrin crumpled against Torin, and the tears she'd held back unleashed in a flood.

"All's well, lass. He's gone."

"So is the traitor on the front steps," Declan's voice carried in the hall. Both Torin and Caitrin lifted their heads. Relief overwhelmed Caitrin at having her husband and her brother coming to her aid. Declan rushed to her other side, hugging her with one arm.

"Let me help you rise. Torin has but one arm at his disposal."

"Torin!" Caitrin was shocked, having momentarily forgotten Torin's crash into the river having just seen him wield his sword so powerfully. "Ye were shot! How are ye here?"

Torin shrugged his uninjured shoulder. "Tis but a flesh wound. 'Tis a match to the one I bear when I served as a shield for Declan's wife. 'Twould seem I am destined to take arrows for the MacCollough women. Do ye ken why the MacCollough men abhor marriage? 'Tis a dangerous proposition, without question."

"Ye are well?" Caitrin pressed, her hand working up the muscles of his arm. "Do ye need care?"

Torin's eyes softened at his wife, now safe and surrounded by her kin. "Davina gave me a field covering after Declan unceremoniously yanked the arrow from my back. The only care I need now is the care ye can give your husband in bed."

Caitrin blushed several shades of rose as the clansmen chuckled and stepped back outside. Declan left his sister's side, telling them not to dawdle in the tower. Torin and Declan shared a hard look before Declan left them alone.

"Ye were strong, lass. Just as I kenned ye could be." He lifted her to her feet with his right arm, holding her tightly against his chest.

"Nay, I'm only strong because ye were here." Her voice dropped to a whisper as they walked to the door.

"Lassie, 'tis untrue. Ye kept your head with ye when ye were taken. And ye kenned what to do when I came here. Ye are stronger than ye believe, lassie. Never doubt that."

He turned her face to his — that strikingly bonny face that spread rumors, captivated kings, and drew the attentions of men and women alike, the face of his wife — and kissed her, his lips soft and yielding and promising more. His strong right arm threaded around her waist, grinding her as close to him as possible. He wanted her, all of her, every part of her beautiful person, but now was not the time.

Releasing her with a twinge of dismay, he hoped she would be ready for more once they returned to their croft.

They stepped out into the night, and Torin directed her away from the limp and bloodied body of Gillivry Ross. Torin and Declan helped her mount Torin's horse, then Torin swung up behind her. His weak arm pulled her against him, sharing his warmth. Caitrin was more than ready to ride home.

Chapter Nineteen: Homecoming

TORIN RODE WITH Caitrin before him, her eyes closed as she tried to forget the horror of the day. Declan rode next to him briefly, telling him about the man on the stairs.

"I kent him from somewhere, I am sure of it."

"The Highlands?" Torin asked.

"I dinna ken. But the world is better off without him. Do ye ken what that scoundrel tried? After siding with the English to abduct your wife, he then tried to barter for his own life. I played the mark, to see what he had to barter with."

"From the look of the man when we left, 'twasn't worth the barter."

Declan chuckled dryly. "Nay, nothing would have been worth it, but the information he provided may well be worthwhile."

"Oh?"

"He confirmed that the health of Longshanks is no' the best – the man is more sickly than the rumors suggest. That information is worth its own weight, and I will share it with the Bruce as soon as we return." Declan's eyes flicked to his sister's peaceful face. "But 'twas nay enough to barter for his life. Nothing would have been. His life was forfeit the minute he took her."

Declan reached out and clasped his sister's hand, and she squeezed his in return. Then he inclined his head at Torin and rode ahead to join John Sinclair and Black Douglas.

The MacCollough and the other men kept their distance for the rest of the journey, granting needed privacy to the overwrought couple. Caitrin let her head fall back onto Torin's chest, the swaying horse lulling her into a contented doze. Even with an injured arm, Torin's embrace remained secure, as though he dreaded losing her again.

"I am glad we found ye safe, Cait," he whispered to her. "I dinna ken how everything got so out of hand. I should have —"

"Nay," Caitrin shushed him, twisting to place her hand on his injured arm. "Ye did everything right. And ye saved me in time. And ye are no' dead. That is enough for tonight." She paused. "I dinna ken what I would have done otherwise."

"Otherwise?" Torin asked. His arms tightened as Caitrin nestled into him.

"Aye. I dinna want to think of such things. I love ye too much for that." Her voice dropped low, almost as if she feared the power of her own words.

"Do ye now?" Torin kept his tone light, but his heart surged and the hair on his arms and chest stood on end at her expression of love.

Caitrin didn't respond but stayed tucked in Torin's embrace. In this moment, with Caitrin in his arms, claiming her love for him, the world seemed perfect. Torin had not felt this happiness in so long. And now that he found such joy, he vowed to never lose it, or her.

"Well, 'tis fortunate, since I love ye, too, lass."

Torin and Declan made sure to find Davina straightaway. A banshee's screech was not as loud as Caitrin's mam when she saw her daughter returned unharmed. Torin held back, waiting for the reunion to end. Declan, conversely, stepped to his mother and his sister, encircling them both with his powerful embrace, grateful to have his family together again.

"I would ye return to *BlackBraes*. I knew 'twas too dangerous here."

"Nay, son," Davina countered, wiping her sleeve across her watery eyes. "We could no' have kenned about the de Lacy lord, or his misguided agreement with Wrexham. 'Tis no more dangerous here with ye than back home, where the English could invade at any moment." Davina shifted her gaze from Torin to Caitrin. "And I would no' have her leave him, ye, or me."

Declan sighed heavily, then nodded at his mother. Not every woman, nor every person for that matter, was as strong a woman as his own wife, the Lady Elayne. And soon enough they would return to *BlackBraes*. That knowledge needed to suffice in these uncertain times.

Caitrin extracted herself from her brother and mother and stepped in front of Torin. The giant stood in a powerful stance, tree-trunk legs spread, and well-muscled arms crossed over his barrel chest. His russet beard and full hair made him seem even larger than life. His darkly serious eyes peered down to catch her light gaze. He was a full Highland warrior, *her* Highland warrior, and Caitrin wanted nothing more than to spend the rest of her life with him.

For now, she was content to spend the night in his bed. She held out her hand, and his gigantic hand enveloped hers. Torin tugged her toward their croft.

"Don't bother us until morning," he quipped with a smile.

Book 5 Excerpt: The Seduction of the Glen

Auchinleck Castle, East Aryshire

ANOTHER VICTORY OVER the English meant even more drinking and celebrating. From his vantage on the second story of the Dumfries keep, he watched his men, the faithful clans of Scotland, sing and cheer, and oh! how the whiskey and ale did flow.

Only King Robert the Bruce didn't celebrate. He sat alone in the second-floor study, a low fire casting fearsome shadows on the wall. He hated what he had to do next, but he had no choice. 'Twas not the same as MacCollough's sister — she was a loyal woman, sister to a loyal man, one of the King's closest advisers. And if MacCollough's sister managed to outsmart the Bruce to wed a clansman she cared for, well, he couldn't fault her for those actions.

But this? This was different. This time 'twas not a loyal woman. 'Twas not the sister of a clansman and close adviser and friend. Aislynn de Valence was the niece of the now defeated Aymer de Valence. She and her sister, Agnes, must be sent north, whether as captives or for future bargaining, the Bruce didn't know. All he did know was he wasn't about to let this asset slip from his fingers.

He flicked his eyes to the door, waiting for the knock. Asper Sinclair would be none too pleased with this assignment, yet 'twas necessary. Someone needed to take the lasses far into Scotland, hide them from the English, and keep their location secret. A brave, honorable man who would keep the lasses safe. And so what if the Bruce was selecting men sworn to bachelorhood as their escorts? If any of the Sinclairs found their way into the hearts of the lasses, matrimony would only solidify the Bruce's position as king.

The sharp rapping at the door finally arrived, and the King bade the man to enter. Asper Sinclair strode in, his head of thick red hair peering around the door before his battle-hardened body followed.

"My King. To what do I owe this honor?" His deep voice rumbled across the shadows of the study. The King kept his eyes on the celebratory men below.

"Dinna call it an honor, yet, Sinclair."

***

Aislynn's slender arms clutched at her sister's more muscular shoulder, trying to shake some sense into the young woman. Though Aislynn was but a year older, and the women resembled each other well, sharing the same light-brown hair and peridot green eyes, sometimes she felt more like a mother than a barely older sister.

And now she pleaded with Agnes, begging her to reconsider as she looked on her sister's costume with horror. Agnes, dressed in a man's dark tunic and baggy brown braies that gathered at her calf and tucked into loose-fitting leather boots, easily passed as a fresh-faced lad.

With her hair hacked off by a dull knife and tucked under a dirty bonnet, Agnes felt secure in her appearance. No man would think her a lass or want to try to wed her. She could move freely across the lowlands before the pretend king could decide her fate, which is exactly what she wanted. Aislynn tried to convince her otherwise.

"Please, Agnes, you will not make it dressed as a boy! You were raised as a lady! Please don't try something so dangerous!"

"Dangerous?" Agnes screeched, her high-pitch causing Aislynn's panicking eyes to flit to the door, certain someone had heard. "'Tis much more dangerous to continue here, and have the Bruce imprison us, or worse! The man is a villain, bent on the destruction of all things English, including us!" Agnes tempered her anger, her face softening at her sister. "Aislynn, I would feel safer if you came with us. Together, we can make it to England, to our uncle, King Edward, and find sanctuary with his court."

Aislynn looked over her shoulder — was someone at the door? "No, please, I've heard the Bruce is considerate, that he —"

"After Uncle Aymer kept the bastard's wife and daughter captive for so long? Do you think he will have any mercy for any de Valence?" She shook her head and yanked her arms away. "No, sister, there's nothing for us here. Look." Agnes tipped her head to the window. "The men are below. We can ride for England. But we must leave now."

Then Aislynn did hear something on the other side of the door. The sound of heavy footfall on stone. Scotsmen were coming down the hall. Aislynn swirled around to face her sister.

"Then you remain here. Let them do with you what they will. I will return with King Edward's army and find you." Agnes lunged toward Aislynn in a quick move, kissing her cheek. "I love you, sister. Look for me to return for you."

Then Agnes was gone, slipping over the windowsill, down a rope made from ripped sheeting the women had torn from the bed. Aislynn leaned out the window, eyes wide with terror as her sister worked her way across the stones and leapt onto the waiting horses below. Two English soldiers, men loyal to Commander Aymer de Valence and the English, followed her, riding off into the dark night. Aislynn sighed and unwrapped the sheet from the bedpost, letting the fabric drop to the dirt of the bailey. The door flung open with a crash, and Aislynn spun around.

"Ye must come with us," the monstrous men in strange skirted clothing commanded, stepping into her chamber. "The Bruce will see ye now."

One man grabbed her arm and hauled her toward the door. The second man peered around the room, on the far side of the sturdy, four-poster bed.

"Where is the other one?" His guttural voice boomed.

Aislynn feigned ignorance and kept her mouth shut. While she may not agree with her sister's actions, she wasn't a traitor. They would have to beat the information out of her.

And as the Scotsmen dragged her toward the study at the far end of the castle, Aislynn paled, praying it wouldn't come to that.

Read the first two books and the prequel to the series:

The Glen Highland Romance Box set

Read book 3: The Exile of the Glen

A Thank You to My Readers

I would like to extend a heartfelt thank you to all of you who continue to read this series. Look for book 5 *The Seduction of the Glen* coming soon!

I cannot write a book without thanking my family, especially my hubby who is so supportive of this writing endeavor. I would also like to thank the amazing writing communities I have had the opportunity to become more involved with. Their continued cheerleading helps on the dry days!

If you liked this book, please leave a review! Reviews can be bread and butter for an author, and I appreciate your comments and feedback.

A HISTORICAL NOTE:

As mentioned in previous books, I do try to remain loyal to the history, but I also bend historical elements for many reasons: to create a stronger setting. With *Jewel,* we finally get to engage with Robert the Bruce in a significant way. While he is not directly the focus of the books, his historic war and subsequent victory over the English to reclaim Scotland provides so many great opportunities to showcase the history. I hope my characters blend right in.

About the Author

Michelle Deerwester-Dalrymple is a professor of writing and an author. She started reading when she was 3 years old, writing when she was 4, and published her first poem at age 16. She has written articles and essays on a variety of topics, including several texts on writing for middle and high school students. Her books include The Glen Highland Romance series: *To Dance in the Glen, The Lady of the Glen*, and *The Exile of the Glen,* with book 4, *The Jewel of the Glen*, releasing soon! She is presently working on a novel inspired by actual events, which she hopes to release by the end of 2019. She lives in California with her family of seven.

Find Michelle Here:

https://linktr.ee/mddalrympleauthor

Also by the Author:

Glen Highland Romance
The Courtship of the Glen –Prequel Short Novella
To Dance in the Glen – Book 1
The Lady of the Glen – Book 2
The Exile of the Glen – Book 3
The Jewel of the Glen – Book 4
The Seduction of the Glen – Book 5
The Warrior of the Glen – Book 6
An Echo in the Glen – Book 7
The Blackguard of the Glen – Book 8 coming soon!

The Celtic Highland Maidens
The Maiden of the Storm
The Maiden of the Grove
The Maiden of the Celts
The Maiden of the Stones – coming soon
The Maiden of the Loch – coming soon

Look for the Fairy Tale Before Series, coming soon!

Historical Fevered Series – short and steamy romance
The Highlander's Scarred Heart
The Highlander's Legacy
The Highlander's Return
Her Knight's Second Chance
The Highlander's Vow
Her Outlaw Highlander
Her Knight's Christmas Gift

As M. D. Dalrymple: Men in Uniform Series

Night Shift – Book 1

Day Shift – Book 2

Overtime – Book 3

Holiday Pay – Book 4

School Resource Officer -- Book 5

Holdover – Book 6 coming soon

Campus Heat Series

Charming – Book 1

Tempting – Book 2

Infatuated – Book 3

Craving – Book 4 – coming soon

Alluring – Book 5 -- coming soon